THE REAL COOL KILLERS

OTHER BOOKS BY CHESTER HIMES
AVAILABLE IN VINTAGE

Cotton Comes to Harlem
The Heat's On

CHESTER HIMES

THE REAL COOL KILLERS

VINTAGE CRIME

VINTAGE BOOKS A DIVISION OF RANDOM HOUSE NEW YORK

FIRST VINTAGE BOOKS EDITION, DECEMBER 1988

 Published in the United States by Random House, Inc., New York. Originally published in France as *Il pleut des coups dur* and in the United States in 1958.

Library of Congress Cataloging-in-Publication Data
Himes, Chester B., 1909–1984
The real cool killers.
I. Title.
PS3515.I713R44 1988 813'.54 88-40121
ISBN 978-0-679-72039-3 (pbk.)

DISPLAY TYPOGRAPHY BY BARBARA M. BACHMAN

Manufactured in the United States of America

146122990

1

"I'm gwine down to de river,
Set down on de ground.
If de blues overtake me,
I'll jump overboard and drown. . ."

Big Joe Turner was singing a rock-and-roll adaptation of *Dink's Blues*. The loud licking rhythm blasted from the jukebox with enough heat to melt bones.

A woman leapt from her seat in a booth as though the music had struck her full of tacks. She was a lean black woman clad in a pink jersey dress and red silk stockings. She pulled up her skirt and began doing a shake dance as though trying to throw off the tacks one by one.

Her mood was contagious. Other women jumped down from their high stools and shook themselves into the act. The customers laughed and shouted and began shaking too. The aisle between the bar and the booths became stormy with shaking bodies.

Big Smiley, the giant-sized bartender, began doing a flat-footed locomotive shuffle up and down behind the bar.

The colored patrons of Harlem's Dew Drop Inn on 129th Street and Lenox Avenue were having the time of their lives that crisp October night.

A white man standing near the middle of the bar watched them with cynical amusement. He was the only white person present.

He was a big man, over six feet tall, dressed in a dark gray flannel suit, white shirt and blood-red tie. He had a big-featured, sallow face with the blotched skin of dissipation. His thick black hair was shot with gray. He held a dead cigar butt between the first two fingers of his left hand. On the third finger was a signet ring. He looked about forty.

The colored women seemed to be dancing for his exclusive entertainment. A slight flush spread over his sallow face.

The music stopped.

A loud grating voice said dangerously above the panting laughter: "Ah feels like cutting me some white mother-raper's throat."

The laughter stopped. The room became suddenly silent.

The man who had spoken was a scrawny little chicken-necked bantamweight, twenty years past his fist-fighting days, with gray stubble tinging his rough black skin. He wore a battered black derby green with age, a ragged plaid mackinaw and blue denim overalls.

His small enraged eyes were as red as live coals. He stalked stiff-legged toward the big white man, holding an open spring-blade knife in his right hand, the blade pressed flat against his overalled leg.

The big white man turned to face him, looking as though he didn't know whether to laugh or get angry. His hand strayed casually to the heavy glass ashtray on the bar.

"Take it easy, little man, and no one will get hurt," he said.

The little knifeman stopped two paces in front of him and said, "Efn' Ah finds me some white mother-raper up here on my side of town trying to diddle my little gals Ah'm gonna cut his throat."

"What an idea," the white man said. "I'm a salesman. I sell that fine King Cola you folks like so much up here. I just dropped in here to patronize my customers."

Big Smiley came down and leaned his ham-sized fists on the bar.

"Looka here, big, bad, and burly," he said to the little knifeman. "Don't try to scare my customers just 'cause you're bigger than they is."

"He doesn't want to hurt anyone," the big white man said. "He just wants some King Cola to soothe his mind.

Give him a bottle of King Cola."

The little knifeman slashed at his throat and severed his red tie neatly just below the knot.

The big white man jumped back. His elbow struck the edge of the bar and the ashtray he'd been gripping flew from his hand and crashed into the shelf of ornamental wine glasses behind the bar.

The crashing sound caused him to jump back again. His second reflex action followed so closely on the the first that he avoided the second slashing of the knife blade without even seeing it. The knot of his tie that had remained was split through the middle and blossomed like a bloody wound over his white collar.

". . . throat cut!" a voice shouted excitedly as though yelling Home Run!

Big Smiley leaned across the bar and grabbed the red-eyed knifeman by the lapels of his mackinaw and lifted him from the floor.

"Gimme that chiv, shorty, 'fore I makes you eat it," he said lazily, smiling as though it were a joke.

The knifeman twisted in his grip and slashed him across the arm. The white fabric of his jacket sleeve parted like a burst balloon and his black-skinned muscles opened like the Red Sea.

Blood spurted.

Big Smiley looked at his cut arm. He was still holding the knifeman off the floor by the mackinaw collar. His eyes had a surprised look. His nostrils flared.

"You cut me, didn't you?" he said. His voice sounding unbelieving.

"Ah'll cut you again," the little knifeman said, wriggling in his grip.

Big Smiley dropped him as though he'd turned hot.

The little knifeman bounced on his feet and slashed at Big Smiley's face.

Big Smiley drew back and reached beneath the bar counter with his right hand. He came up with a short-handled fireman's axe. It had a red handle and a honed, razor-sharp blade.

The little knifeman jumped into the air and slashed at Big Smiley again, matching his knife against Big Smiley's axe.

Big Smiley countered with a right cross with the red-handled axe. The blade met the knifeman's arm in the middle of its stroke and cut it off just below the elbow as though it had been guillotined.

The severed arm in its coat sleeve, still clutching the knife, sailed through the air, sprinkling the nearby spectators with drops of blood, landed on the linoleum tile floor, and skidded beneath the table of a booth.

The little knifeman landed on his feet, still making cutting motions with his half arm. He was too drunk to realize the full impact. He saw that the lower part of his arm had been chopped off; he saw Big Smiley drawing back the red-handled axe. He thought Big Smiley was going to chop at him again.

"Wait a minute, you big mother-raper, till Ah finds my arm!" he yelled. "It got my knife in his hand."

He dropped to his knees and began scrambling about the floor with his one hand, searching for his severed arm. Blood spouted from his jerking stub as though from the nozzle of a hose.

Then he lost consciousness and flopped on his face.

Two customers turned him over; one tied a necktie as a tourniquet about the bleeding arm, the other inserted a chair leg to tighten it.

A waitress and another customer were twisting a knotted towel about Big Smiley's arm. He was still holding the fireman's axe in his right hand, a look of surprise on his face.

The white manager stood on top of the bar and shouted, "Please remain seated, folks. Everybody go back to his seat and pay his bill. The police have been called and everything will be taken care of."

As though he'd fired a starting gun, there was a race for the door.

When Sonny Pickens came out on the sidewalk he saw the big white man looking inside through one of the small front windows.

Sonny had been smoking marijuana cigarettes and he was tree-top high. Seen from his drugged eyes, the dark night sky looked bright purple and the dingy smoke-blackened tenements looked like brand new skyscrapers made of strawberry-colored bricks. The neon signs of the bars and pool rooms and greasy spoons burned like phosphorescent fires.

He drew a blue steel revolver from his inside coat pocket, spun the cylinder and aimed it at the big white man.

His two friends, Rubberlips Wilson and Lowtop Brown, looked at him in pop-eyed amazement. But before either could restrain him, Sonny advanced on the white man, walking on the balls of his feet.

"You there!" he shouted. "You the man what's been messing around with my wife."

The big white man jerked his head about and saw a pistol. His eyes stretched and the blood drained from his sallow face.

"My God, wait a minute!" he cried. "You're making a mistake. All of you folks are confusing me with someone else."

"Ain't going to be no waiting now," Sonny said and pulled the trigger.

Orange flame lanced toward the big white man's chest. Sound shattered the night.

Sonny and the white man leapt simultaneously straight up into the air. Both began running before their feet touched the ground. Both ran straight ahead. They ran head on into one another at full speed. The white man's superior weight knocked Sonny down and he ran over him.

He plowed through the crowd of colored spectators, scattering them like ninepins, and cut across the street through the traffic, running in front of cars as though he didn't see them.

Sonny jumped up to his feet and took out after him. He

ran over the people the big white man had knocked down. Muscles rolled on bones beneath his feet. He staggered drunkenly. Screams followed him and car lights came down on him like shooting stars.

The big white man was moving between parked cars across the street when Sonny shot at him again. He gained the sidewalk safely and began running south along the inner edge.

Sonny followed between the cars and kept after him.

People in the line of fire did acrobatic dives for safety. People up ahead crowded into the doorways to see what was happening. They saw a big white man with wild blue eyes and a stubble of red tie which made him look as though his throat were cut, being chased by a slim black man with a big blue pistol. They drew back out of range.

But the people behind, who were safely out of range, joined the chase.

The white man was in front. Sonny was next. Rubberlips and Lowtop were running at Sonny's heels. Behind them the spectators stretched out in a ragged line.

The white man ran past a group of eight Arabs at the corner of 127th Street. All of the Arabs had heavy, grizzly black beards. All wore bright green turbans, smoke-colored glasses, and ankle-length white robes. Their complexions ranged from stovepipe black to mustard. They were jabbering and gesticulating like a frenzied group of caged monkeys. The air was redolent with the pungent scent of marijuana.

"An infidel!" one yelled.

The jabbering stopped abruptly. They wheeled in a group after the white man.

The white man heard the shout. He saw the sudden movement through the corners of his eyes. He leaped forward from the curb.

A car coming fast down 127th Street burnt rubber in an ear-splitting shriek to keep from running him down.

Seen in the car's headlights, his sweating face was bright

red and muscle-ridged; his blue eyes black with panic; his gray-shot hair in wild disorder.

Instinctively he leaped high and sideways, away from the oncoming car. His arms and legs flew out in grotesque silhouette.

At that instant Sonny came abreast of the Arabs and shot at the leaping white man while he was still in the air.

The orange blast lit up Sonny's distorted face and the roar of the gunshot sounded like a fusillade.

The big white man shuddered and came down limp. He landed face down and in a spread-eagled posture. He didn't get up.

Sonny ran up to him with the smoking pistol dangling from his hand. He was starkly spotlighted by the car's headlights. He looked at the white man lying face down in the middle of the street and started laughing. He doubled over laughing, his arms jerking and his body rocking.

Lowtop and Rubberlips caught up. The eight Arabs joined them in the beams of light.

"Man, what happened?" Lowtop asked.

The Arabs looked at him and began to laugh.

Rubberlips began to laugh too, then Lowtop.

All of them stood in the stark white light, swaying and rocking and doubling up with laughter.

Sonny was trying to say something but he was laughing so hard he couldn't get it out.

A police siren sounded nearby.

2

The telephone rang in the captain's office at the 126th Street precinct station. The uniformed officer behind the desk reached for the outside phone without looking up from behind the record sheet he was filling out.

"Harlem precinct, Lieutenant Anderson," he said.

A high-pitched correct voice said, "Are you the man in charge?"

"Yes, lady," Lieutenant Anderson said patiently and went on writing with his free hand.

"I want to report that a white man is being chased down Lenox Avenue by a colored man with a gun," the voice said with the smug sanctimoniousness of a saved sister.

Lieutenant Anderson pushed aside the record sheet and pulled forward a report pad.

When he'd finished taking down the essential details of her incoherent account, he said, "Thank you, Mrs. Collins," hung up and reached for the closed line to central police on Centre Street.

"Give me the radio dispatcher," he said.

Two colored men were driving east on 135th Street in the wake of a crosstown bus. Shapeless dark hats sat squarely on their clipped kinky hair and their big frames filled up the front seat of a small, battered black sedan.

Static crackled from the shortwave radio and a metallic voice said: "Calling all cars. Riot threatens in Harlem. White man running south on Lenox Avenue at 128th Street. Chased by drunken Negro with gun. Danger of murder."

"Better goose it," the one on the inside said in a grating voice.

"I reckon so," the driver replied laconically.

He gave a short sharp blast on the siren and gunned the small sedan in a crying U-turn in the middle of the block, cutting in front of a taxi coming fast from the direction of The Bronx.

The taxi tore its brakes to keep from ramming into the sedan. Seeing the private license plates, the taxi driver thought they were two small-time hustlers trying to play big shots with the siren on their car. He was an Italian from The Bronx who had grown up with bigtime-gangsters and Harlem hoodlums didn't scare him.

He leaned out of his window and yelled, "You ain't plowing cotton in Mississippi, you black son of a bitch. This is New York City, the Big Apple, where people drive—"

The colored man riding with his girl friend in the back seat leaned quickly forward and yanked at his sleeve. "Man, come back in here and shut yo' mouth," he warned anxiously. "Them is Grave Digger Jones and Coffin Ed Johnson you is talking to. Can't you see that police antenna stuck up from their tail."

"Oh, that's them," the driver said, cooling off as quickly as a showgirl on a broke stud. "I didn't recognize 'em."

Grave Digger had heard him but he mashed the gas without looking around.

Coffin Ed drew his pistol from its shoulder sling and spun the cylinder. Passing street light glinted from the long nickel-plated barrel of the special .38 revolver, and the five brass-jacketed bullets looked deadly in the six chambers. The one beneath the trigger was empty. But he kept an extra box of shells along with his report book and handcuffs in his greased-leather-lined right coat pocket.

"Lieutenant Anderson asked me last night why we stick to these old-fashioned rods when the new ones are so much better. He was trying to sell me on the idea of one of those new hydraulic automatics that shoot fifteen times; said they were faster, lighter and just as accurate. But I told him we'd stick to these."

"Did you tell him how fast you could reload?" Grave Digger carried its mate beneath his left arm.

"Naw, I told him he didn't know how hard these Harlem Negroes' heads are," Coffin Ed said.

His acid-scarred face looked sinister in the dim panel light.

Grave Digger chuckled. "You should have told him that these people don't have any respect for a gun that doesn't have a shiny barrel half a mile long. They want to see what they're being shot with."

"Or else hear it, otherwise they figure it can't do any more damage than their knives."

When they came onto Lenox, Grave Digger wheeled south through the red light with the siren open, passing in front of an eastbound trailer truck, and slowed down behind a sky blue Cadillac Coupe de Ville trimmed in yellow metal, hogging the southbound lane between a bus and a fleet of northbound refrigerator trucks. It had a New York State license plate numbered B-H-21. It belonged to Big Henry who ran the "21" numbers house. Big Henry was driving. His bodyguard, Cousin Cuts, was sitting beside him on the front seat. Two other rugged-looking men occupied the back seat.

Big Henry took the cigar from his thick-lipped mouth with his right hand, tapped ash in the tray sticking out of the instrument panel, and kept on talking to Cuts as though he hadn't heard the siren. The flash of a diamond in his cigar hand lit up the rear window.

"Get him over," Grave Digger said in a flat voice.

Coffin Ed leaned out of the right side window and shot the rear-view mirror off the door hinge of the big Cadillac.

The cigar hand of Big Henry became rigid and the back of his fat neck began to swell as he looked at his shattered mirror. Cuts rose up in his seat, twisting about threateningly, and reached for his pistol. But when he saw Coffin Ed's sinister face staring at him from behind the long nickel-plated barrel of the .38 he ducked like an artful dodger from a hard thrown ball.

Coffin Ed planted a hole in the Cadillac's front fender.

Grave Digger chuckled. "That'll hurt Big Henry more than a hole in Cousin Cut's head."

Big Henry turned about with a look of pop-eyed indignation on his puffed black face, but it sank in like a burst balloon when he recognized the detectives. He wheeled the car frantically toward the curb and crumpled his right front fender into the side of the bus.

Grave Digger had space enough to squeeze through. As they passed, Coffin Ed lowered his aim and shot Big Henry's

gold lettered initials from the Cadillac's door.
"And stay over!" he yelled in a grating voice.
They left Big Henry giving them a how-could-you-do-this-to-me-look with tears in his eyes.
When they came abreast the Dew Drop Inn they saw the deserted ambulance and the crowd running on ahead. Without slowing down, they wormed between the cars parked haphazardly in the street and pushed through the dense jam of people, the sirens shrieking. They dragged to a stop when their headlights focused on the macabre scene.
"Split!" one of the Arabs hissed. "Here's the things."
"The monsters," another chimed.
"Keep cool, fool," the third admonished. "They got nothing on us."
The two tall, lanky, loose-jointed detectives hit the pavement in unison, their nickel-plated .38 specials gripped in their hands. They looked like big-shouldered plowhands in Sunday suits at a Saturday night jamboree.
"Straighten up!" Grave Digger yelled at the top of his voice.
"Count off!" Coffin Ed echoed.
There was movement in the crowd. The morbid and the innocent moved in closer. Suspicious characters began to blow.
Sonny and his two friends turned startled, pop-eyed faces.
"Where they come from?" Sonny mumbled in a daze.
"I'll take him," Grave Digger said.
"Covered," Coffin Ed replied.
Their big flat feet made slapping sounds as they converged on Sonny and the Arabs. Coffin Ed halted at an angle that put them all in line of fire.
Without a break in motion, Grave Digger closed on Sonny and slapped him on the elbow with the barrel of his pistol. With his free hand he caught Sonny's pistol when it flew from his nerveless fingers.
"Got it," he said as Sonny yelped in pain and grabbed his numb arm.

"I ain't–" Sonny tried to finish but Grave Digger shouted, "Shut up!"

"Line up and reach!" Coffin Ed ordered in a threatening voice, menacing them with his pistol. He sounded as though his teeth were on edge.

"Tell the man, Sonny," Lowtop urged in a trembling voice, but it was drowned by Grave Diggers's thundering at the crowd: "Back up!" He lined a shot overhead.

They backed up.

Sonny's good arm shot up and his two friends reached. He was still trying to say something. His Adam's apple bobbed helplessly in his dry wordless throat.

But the Arabs were defiant. They dangled their arms and shuffled about.

"Reach where, man?" one of them said in a husky voice.

Coffin Ed grabbed him by the neck, lifted him off his feet.

"Easy, Ed," Grave Digger cautioned in a strangely anxious voice. "Easy does it."

Coffin Ed halted, his pistol ready to shatter the Arab's teeth, and shook his head like a dog coming out of water. Releasing the Arab's neck, he backed up one step and said in his grating voice: "One for the money . . . and two for the show. . ."

It was the first line of a jingle chanted in the game of hide-and-seek as a warning from the "seeker" to the "hiders" that he was going after them.

Grave Digger took the next line, "Three to get ready. . ."

But before he could finish it with "And here we go," the Arabs had fallen into line with Sonny and had raised their hands high into the air.

"Now keep them up," Coffin Ed said.

"Or you'll be the next ones lying on the ground," Grave Digger added.

Sonny finally got out the words, "He ain't dead. He's just fainted."

"That's right," Rubberlips confirmed. "He ain't been hit. It just scared him so he fell unconscious."

"Just shake him and he'll come to," Sonny added.

The Arabs started to laugh again, but Coffin Ed's sinister face silenced them.

Grave Digger stuck Sonny's revolver into his own belt, holstered his own revolver, and bent down and lifted the white man's face. Blue eyes stared fixedly at nothing. He lowered the head gently and picked up a limp, warm hand, feeling for a pulse.

"He ain't dead," Sonny repeated. But his voice had grown weaker. "He's just fainted, that's all."

He and his two friends watched Grave Digger as though he were Jesus Christ bending over the body of Lazarus.

Grave Digger's eyes explored the white man's back. Coffin Ed stood without moving, his scarred face like a bronze mask cast with trembling hands. Grave Digger saw a black wet spot in the white man's thick gray-shot black hair, low down at the base of the skull. He put his fingertips to it and they came off stained. He straightened up slowly, held his wet fingertips in the white headlights; they showed red. He said nothing.

The spectators crowded nearer. Coffin Ed didn't notice; he was looking at Grave Digger's bloody fingertips.

"Is that blood?" Sonny asked in a breaking whisper. His body began to tremble, coming slowly upward from his grasshopper legs.

Grave Digger and Coffin Ed stared at him, saying nothing.

"Is he dead?" Sonny asked in a terror-stricken whisper. His trembling lips were dust dry and his eyes were turning white in a black face gone gray.

"Dead as he'll ever be," Grave Digger said in a flat toneless voice.

"I didn't do it," Sonny whispered. "I swear 'fore God in heaven."

"He didn't do it," Rubberlips and Lowtop echoed in unison.

"How does it figure?" Coffin Ed asked.

"It figures for itself," Grave Digger said.

"So help me God, boss. I couldn't have done it," Sonny said in a terrified whisper.

Grave Digger stared at him from agate hard eyes and said nothing.

"You gotta believe him, boss, he couldn't have done it," Rubberlips vouched.

"Naw, suh," Lowtops echoed.

"I wasn't trying to hurt him, I just wanted to scare him," Sonny said. Tears were trickling from his eyes.

"It were that crazy drunk man with the knife that started it," Rubberlips said. "Back there in the Dew Drop Inn."

"Then afterwards the big white man kept looking in the window," Lowtop said. "That made Sonny mad."

The detectives stared at him with blank eyes. The Arabs were motionless.

"He's a comedian," Coffin Ed said finally.

"How could I be mad about my old lady," Sonny argued. "I ain't even got any old lady."

"Don't tell me," Grave Digger said in an unrelenting voice, and handcuffed Sonny. "Save it for the judge."

"Boss, listen, I beg you, I swear 'fore God–"

"Shut up, you're under arrest," Coffin Ed said.

3

A police car siren sounded from the distance. It was coming from the east; it started like the wail of an anguished banshee and grew into a scream. Another sounded from the west; it was joined by other from the north and south, one sounding after another like jets taking off from an aircraft carrier.

"Let's see what these real cool Moslems are carrying," Grave Digger said.

"Count off, you sheiks," Coffin Ed said.

They had the case wrapped up before the prowl cars arrived. The pressure was off. They felt cocky.

"Praise Allah," the tallest of the Arabs said.

As though performing a ritual, the others said, "Mecca," and all bowed low with outstretched arms.

"Cut the comedy and straighten up," Grave Digger said. "We're holding you as witnesses."

"Who's got the prayer?" the leader asked with bowed head.

"I've got the prayer," another replied.

"Pray to the great monster," the leader commanded.

The one who had the prayer turned slowly and presented his white-robed backside to Coffin Ed. A sound like a hound dog baying issued from his rear end.

"Allah be praised," the leader said, and the loose white sleeves of their robes fluttered in response.

Coffin Ed didn't get it until Sonny and his friends laughed in amazement. Then his face contorted in black rage.

"Punks!" he grated harshly, somersaulted the bowed Arab with one kick, and leveled on him with his pistol as if to shoot him.

"Easy man, easy," Grave Digger said, trying to keep a straight face. "You can't shoot a man for aiming a fart at you."

"Hold it, monster," a third Arab cried, and flung liquid from a glass bottle toward Coffin Ed's face. "Sweeten thyself."

Coffin Ed saw the flash of the bottle and the liquid flying and ducked as he swung his pistol barrel.

"It's just perfume," the Arab cried in alarm.

But Coffin Ed didn't hear him through the roar of blood in his head. All he could think of was a con man called Hank throwing a glass of acid into his face. And this looked like another acid thrower. Quick scalding rage turned his acid-burnt face into a hideous mask and his scarred lips drew back from his clenched teeth.

He fired two shots together and the Arab holding the half-filled perfume bottle said, "Oh," softly and folded slowly to the pavement. Behind, in the crowd, a woman screamed as her leg gave beneath her.

The other Arabs broke into wild flight. Sonny broke with them. A split second later his friends took off in his wake.

"God damn it, Ed!" Grave Digger shouted and lunged for the gun.

He made a grab for the barrel, deflecting the aim as it went off again. The bullet cut a telephone cable in two overhead. It fell into the crowd, setting off a cacophony of screams.

Everybody ran.

The panic-stricken crowd stampeded for the nearest doorways, trampling the woman who was shot and two others who fell.

Grave Digger grappled with Coffin Ed and they crashed down on top of the dead white man. Grave Digger had Coffin Ed's pistol by the barrel and was trying to wrest it from his grip.

"It's me, Digger, Ed," he kept saying. "Let go the gun."

"Turn me loose, Digger, turn me loose. Let me kill 'im," Coffin Ed mouthed insanely, tears streaming from his hideous face. "They tried it again, Digger."

They rolled over the corpse and rolled back.

"That wasn't acid, that was perfume," Grave Digger said, gasping for breath.

"Turn me loose, Digger, I'm warning you," Coffin Ed mumbled.

While they threshed back and forth over the corpse, two of the Arabs followed Sonny into the doorway of a tenement. The other people crowding into the doorway stepped aside and let them pass. Sonny saw the stairs were crowded and kept on going through, looking for a back exit. He came out onto a small back courtyard, enclosed with stone walls. The Arabs followed him. One put a noose over his head, knocking off his hat, and drew it tight. The other pulled a switch-blade knife and pressed the point against his side.

"If you holler you're dead," the first one said.

The Arab leader joined them.

"Let's get him away from here," he said.

At that moment the patrol cars began to unload. Two harness cops and Detective Haggerty hit the deck and were the first on the murder scene.

"Holy mother!" Haggerty exclaimed.

The cops stared aghast.

It looked to them as though the two colored detectives had the big white man locked in a death struggle.

"Don't just stand there," Grave Digger panted. "Give me a hand."

"They'll kill him," Haggerty said, wrapping his arms about Grave Digger and trying to pull him away. "You grab the other one," he said to the cops.

"To hell with that," the cop said, swinging his black-jack across Coffin Ed's head, knocking him unconscious.

The other cop drew his pistol and took aim at the corpse. "One move out of you and I'll shoot," he said.

"He won't move; he's dead," Grave Digger said to Haggerty.

"Well, Hell," Haggerty said indignantly, releasing him. "You asked me to help. How in hell do I know what's going on?"

Grave Digger shook himself and looked at the third cop. "You didn't have to slug him," he said.

"I wasn't taking no chances," the cop said.

"Shut up and watch the Arab," Haggerty said.

The cop moved over and looked at the Arab. "He's dead, too."

"Holy Mary, the plague," Haggerty said. "Look after that woman then."

Four more cops came running. At Haggerty's order, two turned toward the woman who'd been shot. She was lying in the street, deserted.

"She's alive, just unconscious," the cop said.

"Leave her for the ambulance," Haggerty said.

"Who're you ordering about?" the cop said. "We know our business."

"To hell with you," Haggerty said.

Grave Digger bent over Coffin Ed, lifted his head and put an open bottle of ammonia to his nose. Coffin Ed groaned.

A red-faced uniformed sergeant built like a General Sherman tank loomed above him.

"What happened here?" he asked.

Grave Digger looked up. "A rumpus broke and we lost our prisoner."

"Who shot your partner?"

"He's not shot, he's just knocked out."

"That's all right then. What's your prisoner look like?"

"Black man, about five eleven, twenty-five to thirty years, one-seventy to one-eighty pounds, narrow face sloping down to chin, wearing light gray hat, dark gray hickory-striped suit, white tab collar, red striped tie, beige chukker boots. He's handcuffed."

The sergeant's small china-blue eyes went from the big white corpse to the bearded Arab corpse.

"Which one did he kill?" he asked.

"The white man," Grave Digger said.

"That's all right, we'll get him," he said. Raising his voice, he called, "Professor!"

The corporal who'd stopped to light a cigarette said, "Yeah."

"Rope off this whole goddamned area," the sergeant said. "Don't let anybody out. We want a Harlem-dressed Zulu. Killed a white man. Can't have gotten far 'cause he's handcuffed."

"We'll get 'im," the corporal said.

"Pick up all suspicious persons," the sergeant said.

"Right," the corporal said, hurrying off towards the cops that were just arriving.

"Who shot the Arab?" the sergeant asked.

"Ed shot him," Grave Digger said.

"That's all right then," the sergeant said. "We'll get your prisoner. I'm sending for the lieutenant and the medical examiner. Save the rest for them."

He turned and followed the corporal.

Coffin Ed stood up shakily. "You should have let me killed that son of a bitch, Digger," he said.

"Look at him," Grave Digger said, nodding toward the Arab's corpse.

Coffin Ed stared.

"I didn't even know I hit him," he said as though coming out of a daze. After a moment he added, "I can't feel sorry for him. I tell you, Digger, death is on any son of a bitch who tries to throw acid into my eyes again."

"Smell yourself, man," Grave Digger said.

Coffin Ed bent his head. The front of his dark wrinkled suit reeked with the scent of dime-store perfume.

"That's what he threw. Just perfume," Grave Digger said. "I tried to warn you."

"I must not have heard you."

Grave Digger took a deep breath. "God damn it, man, you got to control yourself."

"Well, Digger, a burnt child fears fire. Anybody who tries to throw anything at me when they're under arrest is apt to get shot."

Grave Digger said nothing.

"What happened to our prisoner?" Coffin Ed asked.

"He got away," Grave Digger said.

They turned in unison and surveyed the scene.

Patrol cars were arriving by the minute, erupting cops as though for an invasion. Others had formed blockades across Lenox Avenue at 128th and 126th Streets, and had blocked off 127th Street on both sides.

Most of the people had gotten off the street. Those that stayed were being arrested as suspicious persons. Several drivers trying to move their cars were protesting their innocence loudly.

The packed bars in the area were being rapidly sealed by

the police. The windows of tenements were jammed with black faces and the exits blocked by police.

"They'll have to go through this jungle with a fine-toothed comb," Grave Digger said. "With all these white cops about, any colored family might hide him."

"I'll want those gangster punks too," Coffin Ed said.

"Well, we'll just have to wait now for the men from homicide."

But Lieutenant Anderson arrived first, with the harness sergeant and Detective Haggerty latched on to him. The five of them stood in a circle in the car's headlights between the two corpses.

"All right, just give me the essential points first," Anderson said. "I put out the flash so I know the start. The man hadn't been killed when I got the first report."

"He was dead when we got here," Grave Digger said in a flat, toneless voice. "We were the first here. The suspect was standing over the victim with the pistol in his hand –"

"Hold it," a new voice said.

A plain-clothes lieutenant and a sergeant from downtown homicide bureau came into the circle.

"These are the arresting officers," Anderson said.

"Where's the prisoner?" the homicide lieutenant asked.

"He got away," Grave Digger said.

"Okay, start over," the homicide lieutenant said.

Grave Digger gave him the first part then, went on:

"There were two friends with him and a group of teenage gangsters around the corpse. We disarmed the suspect and handcuffed him. When we started to frisk the gangster punks we had a rumble. Coffin Ed shot one. In the rumble the suspect got away."

"Now let's get this straight," the homicide lieutenant said.

"Were the teenagers implicated too?"

"No, we just wanted them as witnesses," Grave Digger said. "There's no doubt about the suspect."

"Right."

"When I got here Jones and Johnson were fighting, rolling all over the corpse," Haggerty said. "Jones was trying to disarm Johnson."

Lieutenant Anderson and the men from homicide looked at him, then turned to look at Grave Digger and Coffin Ed in turn.

"It was like this," Coffin Ed said. "One of the punks turned up his ass and farted toward me and –"

Anderson said, "Huh!" and the homicide lieutenant said incredulously, "You killed a man for farting?"

"No, it was another punk he shot," Grave Digger said in his toneless voice. "One who threw perfume on him from a bottle. He thought it was acid the punk was throwing."

They looked at Coffin Ed's acid-burnt face and looked away embarrassedly.

"The fellow who was killed is an Arab," the sergeant said.

"That's just a disguise," Grave Digger said. "They belong to a group of teenage gangsters who call themselves Real Cool Moslems."

"Hah!" the homicide lieutenant said.

"Mostly they fight a teenage gang of Jews from The Bronx," Grave Digger elaborated. "We leave that to the welfare people."

The homicide sergeant stepped over to the Arab corpse and removed the turban and peeled off the artificial beard. The face of a colored youth with slick conked hair and beardless cheeks stared up. He dropped the disguises beside the corpse and sighed.

"Just a baby," he said.

For a moment no one spoke.

Then the homicide lieutenant asked, "You have the homicide gun?"

Grave Digger took it from his pocket, holding the barrel by the thumb and first finger, and gave it to him.

The lieutenant examined it curiously for some moments. Then he wrapped it in his handkerchief and slipped it into his coat pocket.

"Had you questioned the suspect?" he asked.

"We hadn't gotten to it," Grave Digger said. "All we know is the homicide grew out of a rumpus at the Dew Drop Inn."

"That's a bistro a couple of blocks up the street," Anderson said. "They had a cutting there a short time earlier."

"It's been a hot time in the old town tonight," Haggerty said.

The homicide lieutenant raised his brows enquiringly at Lieutenant Anderson.

"Suppose you go to work on that angle, Haggerty," Anderson said. "Look into that cutting. Find out how it ties in."

"We figure on doing that ourselves," Grave Digger said.

"Let him go on and get started," Anderson said.

"Right-o," Haggerty said. "I'm the man for the cutting."

Everybody looked at him. He left.

The homicide lieutenant said, "Well, let's take a look at the stiffs."

He gave each a cursory examination. The teenager had been shot once, in the heart.

"Nothing to do but wait for the coroner," he said.

They looked at the unconscious woman.

"Shot in the thigh, high up," the homicide sergeant said. "Loss of blood but not fatal – I don't think."

"The ambulance will be here any minute," Anderson said.

"Ed shot at the gangster twice," Grave Digger said. "It must have been then."

"Right."

No one looked at Coffin Ed. Instead, they made a pretense of examining the area.

Anderson shook his head. "It's going to be a hell of a job finding your prisoner in this dense slum," he said.

"There isn't any need," the homicide lieutenant said. "If this was the pistol he had, he's as innocent as you and me.

This pistol won't kill anyone." He took the pistol from his pocket and unwrapped it. "This is a thirty-seven caliber blank pistol. The only bullets made to fit it are blanks and they can't be tampered with enough to kill a man. And it hasn't been made over into a zip gun."

"Well," Lieutenant Anderson said at last. "That tears it."

4

There was a rusty sheet-iron gate in the concrete wall between the small back courts. The gang leader unlocked it with his own key. The gate opened silently on oiled hinges.

He went ahead.

"March!" the henchman with the knife ordered, prodding Sonny.

Sonny marched.

The other henchman kept the noose around his neck like a dog chain.

When they'd passed through, the leader closed and locked the gate.

One of the henchman said, "You reckon Caleb is bad hurt?"

"Shut up talking in front of the captive," the leader said. "Ain't you got no better sense than that."

The broken concrete paving was strewn with broken glass bottles, rags and diverse objects thrown from the back windows: a rusty bed spring, a cotton mattress with a big hole burnt in the middle, several worn-out automobile tires, the half-dried carcass of a black cat with its left foot missing and its eyes eaten out by rats.

They picked their way through the debris carefully.

Sonny bumped into a loose stack of garbage cans. One fell with a loud clatter. A sudden putrid stink arose.

"God damn it, look out!" the leader said. "Watch where you're going."

"Aw, man, ain't nobody thinking about us back here," Choo-Choo said.

"Don't call me man," the leader said.

"Sheik, then."

"What you jokers gonna do with me?" Sonny asked.

His weed jag was gone; he felt weak-kneed and hungry; his mouth tasted brackish and his stomach was knotted with fear.

"We're going to sell you to the Jews," Choo-Choo said.

"You ain't fooling me, I know you ain't no Arabs," Sonny said.

"We're going to hide you from the police," Sheik said.

"I ain't done nothing," Sonny said.

Sheik halted and they all turned and looked at Sonny. His eyes were white half moons in the dark.

"All right then, if you ain't done nothing we'll turn you back to the cops," Sheik said.

"Naw, wait a minute, I just want to know where you're taking me."

"We're taking you home with us."

"Well, that's all right then."

There was no back door to the hall as in the other tenement. Decayed concrete stairs led down to a basement door. Sheik produced a key on his ring for that one also. They entered a dark passage. Foul water stood on the broken pavement. The air smelled like molded rags and stale sewer pipes. They had to remove their smoked glasses in order to see.

Halfway along, feeble yellow light slanted from an open door. They entered a small, filthy room.

A sick man clad in long cotton drawers lay beneath a ragged horse blanket on a filthy pallet of burlap sacks.

"You got anything for old Bad-eye," he said in a whining voice.

"We got you a fine black gal," Choo-Choo said.

The old man raised up on his elbows. "Whar she at?"

"Don't tease him," Inky said.

"Lie down and shut," Sheik said. "I told you before we wouldn't have nothing for you tonight." Then to his henchmen, "Come on, you jokers, hurry up."

They began stripping off their disguises. Beneath their white robes they wore sweat shirts and black slacks. The beards were put on with make-up gum.

Without their disguises they looked like three high-school students.

Sheik was a tall yellow boy with strange yellow eyes and reddish kinky hair. He had the broad-shouldered, trim-waisted figure of an athlete. His face was broad, his nose flat with wide, flaring nostrils, and his skin freckled. He looked disagreeable.

Choo-Choo was shorter, thicker and darker, with the egg-shaped head and flat, mobile face of the born joker. He was bowlegged and pigeon-toed but fast on his feet.

Inky was an inconspicuous boy of medium size, with a mild, submissive manner, and black as the ace of spades.

"Where's the gun?" Choo-Choo asked when he didn't see it stuck in Sheik's belt.

"I slipped it to Bones."

"What's he going to do with it?"

"Shut up and quit questioning what I do."

"Where you reckon they all went to, Sheik?" Inky asked, trying to be peacemaker.

"They went home if they got sense," Sheik said.

The old man on the pallet watched them fold their disguises into small packages.

"Not even a little taste of King Kong," he whined.

"Naw, nothing!" Sheik said.

The old man raised up on his elbows. "What do you mean, naw? I'll throw you out of here. I'se the janitor. I'll take my keys away from you. I'll –"

"Shut your mouth before I shut it and if any cops come messing around down here you'd better keep it shut too. I'll have something for you tomorrow."

"Tomorrow? A bottle?"

The old man lay back mollified.

"Come on," Sheik said to the others.

As they were leaving he snatched a ragged army overcoat from a nail on the door without the janitor noticing. He stopped Sonny in the passage and took the noose from about his neck, then looped the overcoat over the handcuffs. It looked as though Sonny were merely carrying an overcoat with both hands.

"Now nobody'll see those cuffs," Sheik said. Turning to Inky, he said, "You go up first and see how it looks. If you think we can get by the cops without being stopped, give us the high sign."

Inky went up the rotten wooden stairs and through the doorway to the ground-floor hall. After a minute he opened the door and beckoned.

They went up in single file.

Strangers who'd ducked into the building to escape the shooting were held there by two uniformed cops blocking the outside doorway. No one paid any attention to Sonny and the three gangsters. They kept on going to the top floor.

Sheik unlocked a door with another key on his ring, and led the way into a kitchen.

An old colored woman clad in a faded blue Mother Hubbard with darker blue patches sat in a rocking chair by a coal-burning kitchen stove, darning a threadbare man's woolen sock on a wooden egg, and smoking a corncob pipe.

"Is that you, Caleb?" she asked, looking over a pair of ancient steel-rimmed spectacles.

"It's just me and Choo-Choo and Inky," Sheik said.

"Oh, it's you, Samson." The very note of expectancy in her voice died in disappointment. "Whar's Caleb?"

"He went to work downtown in a bowling alley, Granny. Setting up pins," Sheik said.

"Lord, that chile is always out working at night," she said with a sigh. "I sho hope God he ain't getting into no trouble with all this night work, 'cause his old Granny is too old to watch over him as a mammy would."

She was so old the color had faded in spots from her dark brown skin so that it looked like the skin of a dried speckled pea, and once-brown eyes had turned milky blue. Her bony cranium was bald at the front and the speckled skin was taut against the skull. What remained of her short gray hair was gathered into a small tight ball at the back of her head. The outline of each finger bone plying the darning needle was plainly visible through the transparent parchment-like skin.

"He ain't getting into no trouble," Sheik said.

Inky and Choo-Choo pushed Sonny into the kitchen and closed the door.

Granny peered over her spectacles at Sonny. "I don't know this boy. Is he a friend of Caleb's too?"

"He's the fellow Caleb is taking his place," Sheik said. "He hurt his hands."

She pursed her lips. "There's so many of you boys coming and going in here all the time I sho hope you ain't getting into no mischief. And this new boy looks older than you others is."

"You worry too much," Sheik said harshly.

"Hannh?"

"We're going on to our room," Sheik said. "Don't wait up for Caleb. He's going to be late."

"Hannh?"

"Come on," Sheik said. "She ain't hearing no more."

It was a shotgun flat, one room opening into the other. The next room contained two small white enameled iron beds where Caleb and his grandmother slept, and a small potbellied stove on a tin mat in one corner. A table held a pitcher and washbowl; there was a small dime-store mirror on top of a chest of drawers. As in the kitchen, everything was spotlessly clean.

"Give me your things and watch out for Granny," Sheik said, taking their bundled-up disguises.

Choo-Choo bent his head to the keyhole.

Sheik unlocked a large old cedar chest with another key

from his ring and stored their bundles beneath layers of old blankets and house furnishings. It was Granny's hope chest; there she stored things given her by the white folks she worked for to give Caleb when he got married. Sheik locked the chest and unlocked the door to the next room. They followed him and he locked the door behind them.

It was the room he and Choo-Choo rented. There was a double bed where he and Choo-Choo slept, chest of drawers and mirror, pitcher and bowl on the table, as in the other room. The corner was curtained off with calico for a closet. But a lot of junk lay around and it wasn't as clean.

A narrow window opened to the platform of the red-painted iron fire escape that ran down the front of the building. It was protected by an iron grille closed by a padlock.

Sheik unlocked the grille and stepped out onto the fire escape.

"Look at this," he said.

Choo-Choo joined him; Inky and Sonny squeezed into the window.

"Watch the captive, Inky," Sheik said.

"I ain't no captive," Sonny said.

"Just look," Sheik said, pointing toward the street.

Below, on the broad avenue, red-eyed prowl cars were scattered thickly, like monster ants about an ant-hill. Three ambulances were threading through the maze, two police hearses, and cars from the police commissioner's office and the medical examiner's office. Uniformed cops and men in plain clothes were coming and going in every direction.

"The men from Mars," Sheik said. "The big dragnet. What you think about that, Choo-Choo?"

Choo-Choo was busy counting.

The lower landings and stairs of the fire escape were packed with other people watching the show. Every front window as far as the eye could see on both sides of the street was jammed with black heads.

"I counted thirty-one prowl cars," Choo-Choo said.

"That's more than was up on Eighth Avenue when Coffin Ed got that acid throwed in his eyes."

"They're shaking down the buildings one by one," Sheik said.

"What we're going to do with our captive?" Choo-Choo asked.

"We got to get the cuffs off first. Maybe we can hide him up in the pigeon's roost."

"Leave the cuffs on him."

"Can't do that. We got to get ready for the shakedown."

He and Choo-Choo stepped back into the room. He took Sonny by the arm, and pointed toward the street.

"They're looking for you, man."

Sonny's black face began graying again.

"I ain't done nothing. That wasn't a real pistol I had. That was a blank gun."

The three of them stared at him disbelievingly.

"Yeah, that ain't what they think," Choo-Choo said.

Sheik was staring at Sonny with a strange expression. "You sure, man?" he asked tensely.

"Sure I'm sure. It wouldn't shoot nothing but thirty-seven caliber blanks."

"Then it wasn't you who shot the big white stud?"

"That's what I been telling you. I couldn't have shot him."

A change came over Sheik. His flat, freckled yellow face took on a brutal look. He hunched his shoulders, trying to look dangerous and important.

"The cops are trying to frame you, man," he said. "We got to hide you now for sure."

"What you doing with a gun that don't shoot bullets?" Choo-Choo asked.

"I keep it in my shine parlor as a gag, is all," Sonny said.

Choo-Choo snapped his fingers. "I know you. You're the joker what works in that shoe shine parlor beside the Savoy."

"It's my own shoe shine parlor."

"How much marijuana you got stashed there?"
"I don't handle it."
"Sheik, this joker's a square."
"Cut the gab," Sheik said. "Let's get these handcuffs off this captive."
He tried keys and lockpicks but he couldn't get them open. So he gave Inky a triangle file and said, "Try filing the chain in two. You and him set on the bed." Then to Sonny, "What's your name, man?"
"Aesop Pickens, but people mostly call me Sonny."
"All right then, Sonny."
They heard a girl's voice talking to Granny and listened silently to rubber-soled shoes crossing the other room.
A single rap, then three quick ones, then another single rap sounded on the door.
"Gaza," Sheik said with his mouth against the panel.
"Suez," a girl's voice replied.
Sheik unlocked the door.
A girl entered and he locked the door behind her.
She was a tall sepia-colored girl with short black curls, wearing a turtle-necked sweater, plaid skirt, bobby socks, and white buckskin shoes. She had a snub nose, wide mouth, full lips, even white teeth, and wide-set brown eyes fringed with long black lashes.
She looked about sixteen years old, and was breathless with excitement.
Sonny stared at her and muttered to himself, "If this ain't it, it'll have to do."
"Hell, it's just Sissie. I thought it was Bones with the gun," Choo-Choo said.
"Stop beefing about the gun. It's safe with Bones. The cops ain't going to shake down no garbage collector's house. His old man works for the city same as they do."
"What's this about Bones and the gun?" Sissie asked.
"Sheik's got –"
"It's none of Sissie's business," Sheik cut him off.
"Somebody said an Arab had been shot and at first I

thought it was you," Sissie said.
"You hoped it was me," Sheik said.
She turned away, blushing.
"Don't look at me," Choo-Choo said to Sheik. "You tell her. She's your girl."
"It was Caleb," Sheik said.
"Caleb! Jesus!" Sissie dropped onto the bed beside Sonny. She looked stunned. "Jesus! Poor little Caleb. What will Granny do?"
"What the hell can she do?" Sheik said brutally. "Raise him from the dead?"
"Does she know?"
"Does it look like she knows?"
"Jesus! Poor little Caleb. What did he do?"
"I gave old Coffin Ed the stink gun and –" Choo-Choo began.
"You didn't!" she exclaimed.
"The hell I didn't."
"What did Caleb do?"
"He threw perfume over the monster. It's the Moslem salute for cops. I told you about it before. But the monster must have thought Cal was throwing some more acid into his eyes. He blasted so fast we couldn't tell him any better."
"Jesus!"
"Where's Sugartit?" Sheik asked.
"At home. She didn't come into town tonight. I phoned her and she said she was sick."
"Yeah. Did you have any trouble getting in here?"
"No. I told the cops at the door that I live here."
They heard the signal rapped on the door.
Sissie gasped.
Sheik looked at her suspiciously. "What the hell's the matter with you?" he asked.
"Nothing."
He hesitated before opening the door. "You ain't expecting nobody?"
"Me? No. Who could I expect?"

"You're acting mighty funny."
"I'm just nervous."
The signal was rapped again.
Sheik stepped to the door and said, "Gaza."
"Suez," a girl's lilting voice replied.
Sheik gave Sissie a threatening look as he unlocked the door.
A small-boned chocolate-brown girl dressed like Sissie slipped hurriedly into the room.
At sight of Sissie she stopped and said, "Oh!" in a guilty tone of voice.
Sheik looked from one to the other. "I thought you said she was at home," he accused Sissie.
"I thought she was," Sissie said.
He turned his gaze on Sugartit. "What the hell's the matter with you? What the hell's going on here?"
"A Moslem's been killed and I thought it was you," she said.
"All you little bitches were hoping it was me," he said.
She had sloe eyes with long black lashes that looked secretive. She threw a quick defiant look at Sissie and said, "Don't include me in that."
"Did you tell Granny?" Sheik asked.
"Of course not."
"It was your lover, Caleb," Sheik said brutally.
She gave a shriek and charged at Sheik, clawing and kicking.
"You dirty bastard!" she cried. "You're always picking at me."
Sissie pulled her off. "Shut up and keep your mouth shut," she said tightly.
"You tell her," Sheik said.
"It was Caleb, all right," Sissie said.
"Caleb!" Sugartit screamed and flung herself face down across the bed. She was up in a flash, hurling accusations at Sheik. "You did it. You got him killed. On account of me. 'Cause he had the best go and you couldn't get me to do

what you made Sissie do."

"That's a lie," Sissie said.

"Caleb!" Sugartit screamed at the top of her voice.

"Shut up, Granny will hear you," Choo-Choo said.

"Granny! Caleb's dead! Sheik killed him!" she screamed again.

"Stop her," Sheik commanded Sissie. "She's getting hysterical and I don't want to have to hurt her."

Sissie clutched her from behind, put one hand over her mouth and twisted her arm behind her back with the other.

Sugartit looked furiously at Sheik over the top of Sissie's hand.

"Granny can't hear," Inky said.

"The hell she can't," Choo-Choo said. "She can hear when she wants to."

"Let me go!" Sugartit mumbled and bit Sissie's hand.

"Stop that!" Sissie said.

"I'm going to him," Sugartit mumbled. "I love him. You can't stop me. I'm going to find out who shot him."

"Your old man shot him," Sheik said brutally. "The monster, Coffin Ed."

"Did I hear someone calling Caleb?" Granny asked from the other side of the door.

Sheik closed his hands quickly about Sugartit's throat and choked her into silence.

"Naw, Granny," he called. "It's just these silly girls arguing about their cubebs."

"Hannh?"

"Cubebs!" Sheik shouted.

"You chillen make so much racket a body can't hear herself think," she muttered.

They heard her shuffling back to the kitchen.

"Jesus, she's sitting up waiting for him," Sissie said.

Sheik and Choo-Choo exchanged glances.

"She don't even know what's happening in the street," Choo-Choo said.

Sheik took his hands away from Sugartit's throat.

5

"How soon can you find out what he was killed with?" the chief of police asked.

"He was killed with a bullet, naturally," the assistant medical examiner said.

"You're not funny," the chief said. "I mean what caliber bullet."

His brogue had begun thickening and the cops who knew him best began getting nervous.

The deputy coroner snapped his bag shut with a gesture of coyness and peered at the chief through magnified eyeballs encircled by black gutta-percha.

"That can't be known until after the autopsy. The bullet will have to be removed from the corpse's brain and subjected to tests –"

The chief listened in red-faced silence.

"I don't perform the autopsy. I'm the night man. I just pass on whether they're dead. I marked this one as D.O.A. That means dead on arrival – my arrival, not his. You know more about whether he was dead on his arrival than I do, and more about how he was killed, too."

"I asked you a civil question."

"I'm giving you a civil answer. Or, I should say, a civil service answer. The men who do the autopsy come on duty at nine o'clock. You ought to get your report by ten."

"That's all I asked you. Thanks. And damn little good that'll do me tonight. And by ten o'clock tomorrow morning the killer ought to be hell and gone to another part of the United States if he's got any sense."

"That's your affair, not mine. You can send the stiffs to the morgue when you've finished with them. I'm finished with them now. Good night, everyone."

No one answered. He left.

"I never knew why we needed a goddamned doctor to tell us whether a stiff was dead or not," the chief grumbled.

He was a big weather-beaten man dressed in a lot of gold braid. He'd come up from the ranks. Everything about him from the armful of gold hash stripes to the box-toed custom-made shoes said "flatfoot." Behind his back the cops on Centre Street called him Spark Plug, after the tender-footed nag in the comic strip "Barney Google."

The group near the white man's corpse, of which he was the hub, had grown by then, to include, in addition to the principals, two deputy police commissioners, an inspector from homicide, and nameless uniformed lieutenants from adjoining precincts.

The deputy commissioners kept quiet. Only the commissioner himself had any authority over the chief, and he was at home in bed.

"This thing's hot as hell," the chief said at large. "Have we got our stories synchronized?"

Heads nodded.

"Come on then, Anderson, we'll meet the press," he said to the lieutenant in charge of the 126th Street precinct station.

They walked across the street to join a group of newsmen who were being held in leash.

"Okay, men, you can get your pictures," he said.

Flash bulbs exploded in his face. Then the photographers converged on the corpses and left him facing the reporters.

"Here it is, men. The dead man has been identified by his paper as Ulysses Galen of New York City. He lives alone in a two-room suite at Hotel Lexington. We've checked that. They think his wife is dead. He's a sales manager for the King Cola Company. We've contacted their main office in Jersey City and learned that Harlem is in his district."

His thick brogue dripped like milk and honey through the noisy night. Stylos scratched on pads. Flash bulbs went off around the corpses like an anti-aircraft barrage.

"A letter in his pocket from a Mrs. Helen Kruger, Wading River, Long Island, begins with Dear Dad. There's an unposted letter addressed to Homer Galen in the sixteen hundred block on Michigan Avenue in Chicago. That's a business district. We don't know whether Homer Galen is his son or another relation –"

"What about how he was killed?" a reporter interrupted.

"We know that he was shot in the back of the head by a Negro man named Sonny Pickens who operates a shoe shine parlor at 134th Street and Lenox Avenue. Several Negroes resented the victim drinking in a bar at 129th Street and Lenox –"

"What was he doing at a crummy bar up here in Harlem?"

"We haven't found that out yet. Probably just slumming. We know that the barman was cut trying to protect him from another colored assailant –"

"How did the shine assail him?"

"This is not funny, men. The first Negro attacked him with a knife – tried to attack him; the bartender saved him. After he left the bar Pickens followed him down the street and shot him in the back."

"You expect him to shoot a white man in the front."

"Two colored detectives from the 126th Street precinct station arrived on the scene in time to arrest Pickens virtually in the act of homicide. He still had the gun in his hand," the chief continued. "They handcuffed the prisoner and were in the act of bringing him in when he was snatched by a teenage Harlem gang that calls itself Real Cool Moslems."

Laughter burst from the reporters.

"What, no Mau-Maus?"

"It's not funny, men," the chief said again. "One of them tried to throw acid in one of the detective's eyes."

The reporters were silenced.

"Another gangster threw acid in an officer's face up here about a year ago, wasn't it?" a reporter said. "He was a colored cop, too. Johnson, Coffin Ed Johnson, they called him."

"It's the same officer," Anderson said, speaking for the first time.

"He must be a magnet," the reporters said.

"He's just tough and they're scared of him," Anderson said. "You've got to be tough to be a colored cop in Harlem. Unfortunately, colored people don't respect colored cops unless they're tough."

"He shot and killed the acid thrower," the chief said.

"You mean the first one or this one?" the reporter asked.

"This one, the Moslem," Anderson said.

"During the excitement, Pickens and the others escaped into the crowd," the chief said.

He turned and pointed toward a tenement building across the street. It looked indescribably ugly in the glare of a dozen powerful spotlights. Uniformed police stood on the roof, others were coming and going through the entrance; still others stuck their heads out of front windows to shout to other cops in the street. The other front windows were jammed with colored faces, looking like clusters of strange purple fruit in the stark white light.

"You can see for yourselves we're looking for the killer," the chief said. "We're going through those buildings with a fine-toothed comb, one by one, flat by flat, room by room. We have the killer's description. He's wearing toolproof handcuffs. We should have him in custody before morning. He'll never get out of that dragnet."

"If he isn't already out," a reporter said.

"He's not out. We got here too fast for that."

The reporters then began to question him.

"Is Pickens one of the Real Cool Moslems?"

"We know he was rescued by seven of them. The eighth was killed."

"Was there any indication of robbery?'"

"Not unless the victim had valuables we don't know about. His wallet, watch and rings are intact."

"Then what was the motive? A woman?"

"Well, hardly. He was an important man, well off financially. He didn't have to chase up here."

"It's been done before."

The chief spread his hands. "That's right. But in this case both Negroes who attacked him did so because they resented his presence in a colored bar. They expressed their resentment in so many words. We have colored witnesses who heard them. Both Negroes were intoxicated. The first had been drinking all evening. And Pickens had been smoking marijuana also."

"Okay, chief, it's your story," the dean of the police reporters said, calling a halt.

The chief and Anderson recrossed the street to the silent group.

"Did you get away with it?" one of the deputy commissioners asked.

"God damn it, I had to tell them something," the chief said defensively. "Did you want me to tell them that a fifteen-thousand-dollar-a-year white executive was shot to death on a Harlem street by a weedhead Negro with a blank pistol who was immediately rescued by a gang of Harlem juvenile delinquents while all we got to show for the efforts of the whole god-damned police force is a dead adolescent who's called a Real Cool Moslem?"

"Sho' 'nuff cool now," Haggerty slipped in *sotto voce*.

"You want us to become the laughing stock of the whole goddamned world," the chief continued, warming up to the subject. "You want it said the New York City police stood by helpless while a white man got himself killed in the middle of a crowded nigger street?"

"Well, didn't he?" the homicide lieutenant said.

"I wasn't accusing you," the deputy commissioner said apologetically.

"Pickens is the one it's rough on," Anderson said. "We've got him branded as a killer when we know he didn't do it."

"We don't know any such goddamned thing," the chief

said, turning purple with rage. "He might have rigged the blanks with bullets. It's been done, God damn it. And even if he didn't kill him, he hadn't ought to've been chasing him with a goddamned pistol that sounded as if it was firing bullets. We haven't got anybody to work on but him and it's just his black ass."

"Somebody shot him, and it wasn't with any blank gun," the homicide lieutenant said.

"Well, God damn it, go ahead and find out who did it!" the chief roared. "You're on homicide; that's your job."

"Why not one of the Moslems," the deputy commissioner offered helpfully. "They were on the scene, and these teenage gangsters always carry guns."

There was a moment of silence while they considered this.

"What do you think, Jones?" the chief asked Grave Digger. "Do you think there was any connection between Pickens and the Moslems?"

"It's like I said before," Grave Digger said. "It didn't look to me like it. The way I figure it, those teenagers gathered around the corpse directly after the shooting, like everybody else was doing. And when Ed began shooting, they all ran together, like everybody else. I see no reason to believe that Pickens even knows them."

"That's what I gathered too," the chief said disappointedly.

"But this is Harlem," Grave Digger amended. "Nobody knows all the connections here."

"Furthermore, we don't have but one of them and that one isn't carrying a gun," Anderson said. "And you've heard Haggerty's report on the statement he took from the bartender and the manager of the Dew Drop Inn. Both Pickens and the other man resented Galen making passes at the colored women. And none of the Moslem gang were even there at the time."

"It could have been some other man feeling the same way," Grave Digger said. "He might have seen Pickens shooting at Galen and thought he'd get in a shot, too."

"These people!" the chief said. "Okay, Jones, you begin to work on that angle and see what you can dig up. But keep it from the press."

As Grave Digger started to walk away, Coffin Ed fell in beside him.

"Not you, Johnson," the chief said. "You go home."

Both Grave Digger and Coffin Ed turned and faced the silence.

"Am I under suspension?" Coffin Ed asked in a grating voice.

"For the rest of the night," the chief said. "I want you both to report to the commissioner's office at nine o'clock tomorrow morning. Jones, you go ahead with your investigation. You know Harlem, you know where you have to go, who to see." He turned to Anderson. "Have you got a man to work with him?"

"Haggerty," Anderson offered.

"I'll work alone," Grave Digger said.

"Don't take any chances," the chief said. "If you need help, just holler. Bear down hard. I don't give a goddamn how many heads you crack; I'll back you up. Just don't kill any more juveniles."

Grave Digger turned and walked with Coffin Ed to their car.

"Drop me at the Independent Subway," Coffin Ed said.

Both of them lived in Jamaica and rode the E train when they didn't use the car.

"I saw it coming," Grave Digger said.

"If it had happened earlier I could have taken my daughter to a movie," Coffin Ed said. "I see so little of her it's getting so I hardly know her."

6

"Let her loose now," Sheik said.

Sissie let her go.

"I'll kill him!" Sugartit raved in a choked voice. "I'll kill him for that!"

"Kill who?" Sheik asked, scowling at her.

"My father. I hate him. The ugly bastard. I'll steal his pistol and shoot him."

"Don't talk like that," Sissie said. "That's no way to talk about your father."

"I hate him, the dirty cop!"

Inky looked up from the handcuffs he was filing. Sonny stared at her.

"Shut up," Sissie said.

"Let her go ahead and croak him," Sheik said.

"Stop picking on her," Sissie said.

Choo-Choo said, "They won't do nothing to her for it. All she got to say is her old man beat her all the time and they'll start crying and talking 'bout what a poor mistreated girl she is. They'll take one look at Coffin Ed and believe her."

"They'll give her a medal," Sheik said.

"Those old welfare biddies will find her a fine family to live with. She'll have everything she wants. She won't have to do nothing but eat and sleep and go to the movies and ride around in a big car," Choo-Choo elaborated.

Sugartit flung herself across the foot of the bed and burst into loud sobs.

"It'll save us the trouble," Sheik said.

Sissie's eyes widened. "You wouldn't!" she said.

"You want to bet we wouldn't?"

"If you keep talking like that I'm going to quit."

Sheik gave her a threatening look. "Quit what?"

"Quit the Moslems."

"The only way you can quit the Moslems is like Caleb quit," Sheik said.

"If I'd ever thought that poor little Caleb –"

Sheik cut her off. "I'll kill you myself."

"Aw, Sheik, she don't mean nothing," Choo-Choo said nervously. "Why don't you light up a couple of sticks and let us Islamites fly to Mecca."

"And let the cops smell it when they shake us down and take us all in. Where are your brains at?"

"We can go up on the roof."

"There're cops on the roof, too."

"On the fire escape then. We can close the window."

Sheik gave it grave consideration. "Okay, on the fire escape. I ain't got but two left and we got to get rid of them anyway."

"I'm going to look and see where the cops is at by now," Choo-Choo said, putting on his smoked glasses.

"Take those cheaters off," Sheik said. "You want the cops to identify you?"

"Aw hell, Sheik, they couldn't tell me from nobody else. Half the cats in Harlem wear their smoke cheaters all night long."

"Go 'head and take a gander at the avenue. We ain't got all night," Sheik said.

Choo-Choo started climbing out the window.

At that moment the links joining the handcuffs separated with a small clinking sound beneath Inky's file.

"Sheik, I've got 'em filed in two," Inky said triumphantly.

"Let's see."

Sonny stood up and stretched his arms.

"Who's he?" Sissie asked as though she'd noticed him for the first time.

"He's our captive," Sheik said.

"I ain't no captive," Sonny said. "I just come with you 'cause you said you was gonna hide me."

Sissie looked round-eyed at the severed handcuffs dangling from the wrists. "What did he do?" she asked.

"He's the gangster who killed the syndicate boss," Sheik said.

Sugartit stopped sobbing abruptly and rolled over and looked up at Sonny through wide wet eyes.

"Was that who he is?" Sissie asked in an awed tone. "The man who was killed, I mean."

"Sure. Didn't you know?" Sheik said.

"I done told you I didn't kill him," Sonny said.

"He claims he had a blank gun," Sheik said. "He's just trying to build up his defense. But the cops know better."

"It was a blank gun," Sonny said.

"What did he kill him for?" Sissie asked.

"They're having a gang war and he got assigned by the Brooklyn mob to make the hit."

"Oh, go to hell," Sissie said.

"I ain't killed nobody," Sonny said.

"Shut up," Sheik said. "Captives ain't allowed to talk."

"I'm getting tired of that stuff," Sonny said.

Sheik looked at him threateningly. "You want us to turn you over to the cops?"

Sonny backtracked quickly. "Naw, Sheik, but hell, ain't no need of taking advantage of me –"

Choo-Choo stuck his head in the window and cut him off: "Cops is out here like white on rice. Ain't nothing but cops."

"Where they at now?" Sheik asked.

"They're everywhere, but right now they's taking the house two doors down. They got all kinds of spotlights turned on the front of the house and cops is walking around down the street with machine guns. We better hurry if we're going to move the prisoner."

"Keep cool, fool," Sheik said. "Take a look at the roof."

"Praise Allah," Choo-Choo said, backing away on his hands and knees.

"Get out of that coat and shirt," Sheik ordered Sonny.

When Sonny had stripped to his underwear shirt, Sheik

looked at him and said, "Nigger, you sure are black. When you was a baby your mama must'a had to chalk your mouth to tell where to stick it."

"I ain't no blacker than Inky," Sonny said defensively.

"I ain't in that," Inky said.

Sheik grinned at him derisively. "You didn't have no trouble, did you, Inky? Your mama used luminous paint on you."

"Come on, man, I'm getting cold," Sonny said.

"Keep your pants on," Sheik said. "Ladies present."

He hung Sonny's coat with his own clothes on the wire line behind the curtain and threw the shirt in the corner. Then he tossed Sonny an old faded red turtle-necked sweater.

"Pull the sleeves down over the irons and put on that there overcoat," he directed, indicating the old army coat he'd taken from the janitor.

"It's too hot," Sonny protested.

"You gonna do what I say, or do I have to slug you?"

Sonny put on the coat.

Sheik then took a pair of leather driving gauntlets from his pasteboard suitcase beneath the bed and handed them to Sonny, too.

"What am I gonna do with these?" Sonny asked.

"Just put them on and shut up, fool," Sheik said.

He then took a long bamboo pole from behind the bed and began passing it through the window. On one end was attached a frayed felt New York Giants pennant.

Choo-Choo came down the fire escape in time to take the pole and lean it against the ladder.

"Ain't no cops on this roof yet but the roof down where they's shaking down is lousy with 'em," he reported.

His face was shiny with sweat and the whites of his eyes had begun to glow.

"Don't chicken out on me now," Sheik said.

"I just needs some pot to steady my nerves."

"Okay, we're going to blow two now." Sheik turned to

Sonny and said, "Outside, boy."

Sonny gave him a look, hesitated, then climbed out on the fire-escape landing.

"Let me come, too," Sissie said.

Sugartit sat up with sudden interest.

"I want both you little jailbaits to stay right here in this room and don't move," Sheik ordered in a hard voice, then turned to Inky, "You come on, Inky, I'm gonna need you."

Inky joined the others on the fire escape. Sheik came last and closed the window. They squatted in a circle. The landing was crowded.

Sheik took two limp cigarettes from the roll of his sweat-shirt and stuck them into his mouth.

"Bombers!" Choo-Choo exclaimed. "You've been holding out on us."

"Give me some fire and less of your lip," Sheik said.

Choo-Choo flipped a dollar lighter and lit both cigarettes. Sheik sucked the smoke deep into his lungs, then passed one of the sticks to Inky.

"You and Choo-Choo take halvers and me and the captive will split this one."

Sonny raised both gloved hands in a pushing gesture. "Pass me. That gage done got me into more trouble now than I can get out of."

"You're chicken," Sheik said contemptuously, sucking another puff. He swallowed back the smoke each time it started up from his lungs. His face swelled and began darkening with blood as the drug took hold. His eyes became dilated and his nostrils flared.

"Man, if I had my heater I bet I could shoot that sergeant down there dead between the eyes," he said. The cigarette was stuck to his bottom lip and dangled up and down when he talked.

"What I'd rather have me is one of those hard-shooting long-barreled thirty-eights like Grave Digger and Coffin Ed have got," Choo-Choo said. "Them heaters can kill a rock. Only I'd want me a silencer on it and I could sit here and pick off any mother-raper I wanted. But I wouldn't shoot nobody unless he was a big shot or the chief of police or somebody like that."

"You're talking about rathers, what you'd rather have; me, I'm talking about facts," Sheik said, the cigarette bobbing up and down.

"What you're talking about will get you burnt up in Sing-Sing if you don't watch out," Choo-Choo said.

"What you mean!" Sheik said, jumping to his feet threateningly. "You're going to make me throw your ass off this fire escape."

Choo-Choo jumped to his feet, too, and backed against the rail. "Throw whose ass off where? This ain't Inky you're talking to. My ass ain't made of chicken feathers."

Inky scrambled to his feet and stepped between them. "What about the captive, Sheik?" he asked in alarm.

"Damn the captive!" Sheik raved and whipped out a bone-handled knife, shaking open the six-inch blade with the same motion.

"Don't cut 'em!" Inky cried.

He knocked Inky into the iron steps with a back-handed slap and grabbed a handful of Choo-Choo's sweat shirt collar.

"You blab and I'll cut your mother-raping throat," he said.

Violence surged through him like runaway blood.

Choo-Choo's eyes turned three-quarters white and a feverish sweat popped out on his dark brown skin.

"I didn't mean nothing, Sheik," he whined desperately, talking low. "You know I didn't mean nothing. A man can talk 'bout his rathers, can't he?"

The violence receded but Sheik was still gripped in a murderous compulsion.

"If I thought you'd pigeon I'd kill you."

"You know I ain't gonna pigeon, Sheik. You know me better than that."

Sheik let go of his collar. Choo-Choo took a deep sighing

breath.

Inky straightened up and rubbed his bruised shin. "You done made me lose the stick," he complained.

"Hell with the stick," Sheik said.

"That's what I mean," Sonny said. "This here gage they sells now will make you cut your own mamma's throat. They must be mixing it with loco weed or somethin'."

"Shut up!" Sheik said, still holding the open knife in his hand. "I ain't gonna tell you no more."

Sonny cast a look at the knife and said, "I ain't saying nothing."

"You better not," Sheik said. Then he turned to Inky. "Inky, you take the captive up on the roof and you and him start flying Caleb's pigeons. You, Sonny, when the cops come you tell them your name is Caleb Bowee and you're just trying to teach your pigeons how to fly at night. You got that?"

"Yeah," Sonny said skeptically.

"You know how to make pigeons fly?"

Sonny hesitated. "Chunk rocks at 'em?"

"Hell, nigger, your brain ain't big as a mustard seed. You can't chunk no rocks up there with all those cops about. What you got to do is take this pole and wave the end with the flag at 'em every time they try to light."

Sonny looked at the bamboo pole skeptically. "S'posin' they fly away and don't come back."

"They ain't going nowhere. They just fly in circles trying all the time to get back into the coop." Sheik doubled over suddenly and started laughing. "Pigeons ain't got no sense, man."

The rest of them just looked at him.

Finally Inky asked, "What you want me to do?"

Sheik straightened up quickly and stopped laughing. "You guard the captive and see that he don't escape."

"Oh!" Inky said. After a moment he asked, "What I'm gonna tell the cops when they ask me what I'm doin'?"

"Hell, you tell the cops Caleb is teaching you how to train

pigeons."

Inky bent over and started rubbing his shins again. Without looking up he said, "You reckon the cops gonna fall for that, Sheik? You reckon they gonna be crazy enough to believe anybody's gonna be flying pigeons with all this going on all around here?"

"Hell, these is white cops," Sheik said contemptuously. "They believe spooks are crazy anyway. You and Sonny just act kind of simpleminded. They gonna to swallow it like it's chocolate ice cream. They ain't going to do nothing but kick you in the ass and laugh like hell about how crazy spooks are. They gonna go home and tell their old ladies and everybody they see about two simpleminded spooks up on the roof teaching pigeons how to fly at night all during the biggest dragnet they ever had in Harlem. You see if they don't."

Inky kept on rubbing his shin. "It ain't that I doubt you, Sheik, but s'posin' they don't believe it."

"God damn it, go ahead and do what I told you and don't stand there arguing with me," Sheik said, hit by another squall of fury. "I'd take me one look at you and this nigger here and I'd believe it myself, and I ain't even no gray cop."

Inky turned reluctantly and started up the stairs toward the roof. Sonny gave another sidelong look at Sheik's open knife and started to follow.

"Wait a minute, simple, don't forget the pole," Sheik said. "I've told you not to try chunking rocks at those pigeons. You might kill one and then you'd have to eat it." He doubled over laughing at his joke.

Sonny picked up the pole with a sober face and climbed slowly after Inky.

"Come on," Sheik said to Choo-Choo, "open the window and let's get back inside."

Before turning his back and bending to open the window, Choo-Choo said, "Listen, Sheik, I didn't mean nothing by that."

"Forget it," Sheik said.

Sissie and Sugartit were sitting silently side by side on the bed, looking frightened and dejected. Sugartit had stopped crying but her eyes were red and her cheeks stained.

"Jesus Christ, you'd think this is a funeral," Sheik said.

No one replied. Choo-Choo fidgeted from one foot to the other.

"I want you chicks to wipe those sad looks off your faces," Sheik said. "We got to look like we're balling and ain't got a thing to worry about when the cops get here."

"*You* go ahead and ball by yourself," Sissie said.

Sheik lunged forward and slapped her over on her side.

She got up without a word and walked to the window.

"If you go out that window I'll throw you down on the street," Sheik threatened.

She stood looking out the window with her back turned and didn't answer.

Sugartit sat quietly on the edge of the bed and trembled.

"Hell," Sheik said disgustedly and flopped lengthwise behind Sugartit on the bed.

She got up and went to stand in the window beside Sissie.

"Come on, Choo-Choo, to hell with those bitches," Sheik said. "Let's decide what to do with the captive."

"Now you're getting down to the gritty," Choo-Choo said enthusiastically, straddling a chair. "You got any plans?"

"Sure. Give me a butt."

Choo-Choo fished two Camels from a squashed package in his sweat shirt roll and lit them, passing one to Sheik.

"This square weed on top of gage makes you crazy," he said.

"Man, my head already feels like it's going to pop open, it's so full of ideas," Sheik said. "If I had me a real mob like Dutch Schultz's I could take over Harlem with the ideas I got. All I need is just the mob."

"Hell, you and me could do it alone," Choo-Choo said.

"We'd need some arms and stuff, some real factory-made heaters and a couple of machine guns and maybe some pineapples."

"If we croaked Grave Digger and the Monster we'd have

two real cool heaters to start off with," Choo-Choo suggested.

"We ain't going to mess with those studs until after we're organized," Sheik said. "Then maybe we can import some talent to make the hit. But we'd need some dough."

"Hell, we can hold the prisoner for ransom," Choo-Choo said.

"Who'd ransom that nigger," Sheik said. "I bet even his own mamma wouldn't pay to get him back."

"He can ransom hisself," Choo-Choo said. "He got a shine parlor, ain't he? Shine parlors make good dough. Maybe he's got a chariot too."

"Hell, I knew all along he was valuable," Sheik said. "That's why I had us snatch him."

"We can take over his shine parlor," Choo-Choo said.

"I got some other plans too," Sheik said. "Maybe we can sell him to the Stars of David for some zip guns. They got lots of zip guns and they're scared to use them."

"We could do that or we could swap him to the Puerto Rican Bandits for Burrhead. We promised Burrhead we'd pay his ransom and they been saying if we don't hurry up and get 'im they're gonna cut his throat."

"Let 'em cut the black mother-raper's throat," Sheik said. "That chicken-hearted bastard ain't no good to us."

"I tell you what, Sheik," Choo-Choo said exuberantly. "We could put him in a sack like them ancient cats like the Dutchman and them used to do and throw him into the Harlem river. I've always wanted to put some bastard into a sack."

"You know how to put a mother-raper into a sack?" Sheik asked.

"Sure, you –"

"Shut up, I'm gonna to tell you how. You knock the mother-raper unconscious first; that's to keep him from jumping about. Then you put a noose with a slip-knot 'round his neck. Then you double him up into a Z and tie the other end of the wire around his knees. Then when you put him in the gunny sack you got to be sure it's big enough to give him some space to move around in. When the mother-raper wakes up and tries to straighten out he chokes hisself to death. Ain't nobody killed 'im. The mother-raper has just committed suicide." Sheik rolled with laughter.

"You got to tie his hands behind his back first," Choo-Choo said.

Sheik stopped laughing and his face became livid with fury. "Who don't know that, fool!" he shouted. " 'Course you got to tie his hands behind his back. You trying to tell me I don't know how to put a mother-raper into a sack. I'll put *you* into a sack."

"I know you know how, Sheik," Choo-Choo said hastily. "I just didn't want you to forget nothing when we put the captive in a sack."

"I ain't going to forget nothing," Sheik said.

"When we gonna put him in a sack?" Choo-Choo asked. "I know where to find a sack."

"Okay, we'll put him in a sack just soon as the police finish here; then we take him down and leave him in the basement," Sheik said.

7

Grave Digger flashed his badge at the two harness bulls guarding the door and pushed inside the Dew Drop Inn.

The joint was jammed with colored people who'd seen the big white man die, but nobody seemed to be worrying about it.

The jukebox was giving out with a stomp version of "Big-Legged Woman." Saxophones were pleading; the horns were teasing; the bass was patting; the drums were chatting; the piano was catting, laying and playing the jive, and a husky female voice was shouting:

". . . you can feel my thigh
But don't you feel up high."

Happy-tail women were bouncing out of their dresses on the high bar stools.

Grave Digger trod on the sawdust sprinkled over the bloodstains that wouldn't wash off and parked on the stool at the end of the bar.

Big Smiley was serving drinks with his left arm in a sling.

The white manager, the sleeves of his tan silk shirt rolled up, was helping.

Big Smiley shuffled down the wet footing and showed Grave Digger most of his big yellow teeth.

"Is you drinking, Chief, or just sitting and thinking?"

"How's the wing?" Grave Digger asked.

"Favorable. It wasn't cut deep enough to do no real damage."

The manager came down and said, "If I'd thought there was going to be any trouble I'd have called the police right away."

"What do you calculate as trouble in this joint?" Grave Digger asked.

The manager reddened. "I meant about the white man getting killed."

"Just what started all the trouble in here?"

"It wasn't exactly what you'd call trouble, Chief," Big Smiley said. "It was only a drunk attacked one of my white customers with his shiv and naturally I had to protect my customer."

"What did he have against the white man?"

"Nothing, Chief. Not a single thing. He was sitting over there drinking one shot of rye after another and looking at the white man standing here tending to his own business. Then he gets red-eyed drunk and his evil tells him to get up and cut the man. That's all. And naturally I couldn't let him do that."

"He must have had some reason. You're not trying to tell me he got up and attacked the man without any reason whatever."

"Naw suh, Chief, I'll bet my life he ain't had no reason at

all to wanta cut the man. You know how our folks is, Chief; he was just one of those evil niggers that when they get drunk they start hating white folks and get to remembering all the bad things white folks ever done to them. That's all. More than likely he was mad at some white man that done something bad to him twenty years ago down South and he just wanted to take it out on this white man in here. It's like I told that white detective who was in here, this white man was standing here at the bar by hisself and that nigger just figgered with all those colored folk in here he could cut him and get away with it."

"Maybe. What's his name?"

"I ain't ever seen that nigger before tonight, Chief; I don't know what is his name."

A customer called from up the bar, "Hey, boss, how about a little service up here?"

"If you want me, Jones, just holler," the manager said, moving off to serve the customer.

"Yeah," Grave Digger said, then asked Big Smiley, "Who was the woman?"

"There she is," Big Smiley said, nodding toward a booth.

Grave Digger turned his head and scanned her.

The black lady in the pink jersey dress and red silk stockings was back in her original seat in a booth surrounded by three workers.

"It wasn't on account of her," Big Smiley added.

Grave Digger slid from his stool, went over to her booth and flashed his badge. "I want to talk to you."

She looked at the gold badge and complained, "Why don't you folks leave me alone? I done already told a white cop everything I know about that shooting, which ain't nothing."

"Come on, I'll buy you a drink," Grave Digger said.

"Well, in that case . . ." she said and went with him to the bar.

At Grave Digger's order Big Smiley grudgingly poured her a shot of gin and Grave Digger said, "Fill it up."

Big Smiley filled the glass and stayed there to listen.

"How well did you know the white man?" Grave Digger asked the lady.

"I didn't know him at all. I'd just seen him around here once or twice."

"Doing what –"

"Just chasing."

"Alone?"

"Yeah."

"Did you see him pick up anyone?"

"Naw, he was one of those particular kind. He never saw nothing he liked."

"Who was the colored man who tried to cut him?"

"How the hell should I know?"

"He wasn't a relative of yours?"

"A relation of mine. I should hope not."

"Just exactly what did he say to the white man when he started to attack him?"

"I don't remember exactly; he just said something 'bout him messing about with his gal."

"That's the same thing the other man, Sonny Pickens, accused him of."

"I don't know nothing about that."

He thanked her and wrote down her name and address.

She went back to her seat.

He returned back to Big Smiley. "What did Pickens and the man argue about?"

"They ain't had no argument, Chief. Not in here. It wasn't on account of nothing that happened in here that he was shot."

"It was on account of something," Grave Digger said. "Robbery doesn't figure, and people in Harlem don't kill for revenge."

"Naw suh, leastwise they don't shoot."

"More than likely they'll throw acid or hot lye," Grave Digger said.

"Naw, suh, not on no white gennelman."

"So what else is there left but a woman," Grave Digger said.

"Naw suh," Big Smiley contradicted flatly. "You know better'n that, Chief. A colored woman don't consider diddling with a white man as being unfaithful. They don't consider it no more than just working in service, only they is getting better paid and the work is less straining. 'Sides which, the hours is shorter. And they old men don't neither. Both she and her old man figger it's like finding money in the street. And I don't mean no cruisers neither; I means church people and Christians and all the rest."

"How old are you, Smiley?" Grave Digger asked.

"I be forty-nine come December seventh."

"You're talking about old times, son. These young colored men don't go in for that slavery-time deal anymore."

"Shucks, Chief, you just kidding. This is old Smiley. I got dirt on these women in Harlem ain't never been plowed. Shucks, you and me both can put our finger on high society colored ladies here who got their whole rep just by going with some big important white man. And their old men is cashing in on it, too; makes them important, too, to have their old ladies going with some big-shot gray. Shucks, even a hard-working nigger wouldn't shoot a white man if he come home and found him in bed with his old lady with his pants down. He might whup his old lady just to show her who was boss, after he done took the money 'way from her, but he wouldn't sure 'nough hurt her like he'd do if he caught her screwing some other nigger."

"I wouldn't bet on it," Grave Digger said.

"Have it your own way, Chief, but I still think you're barking up the wrong tree. Lissen, the only way I figger a colored man in Harlem gonna kill a white man is in a fight. He'll draw his shiv if he getting his ass whupped and maybe stab him to death. But I'll bet my life ain't no nigger up here gonna shoot down no white man in cold blood – no important white gennelman like him."

"Would the killer have to know he was important?"

"He'd know it," Big Smiley said positively.

"You knew him?" Grave Digger said.

"Naw suh, not to say knew him. He come in here two, three times before but I didn't know his name."

"You expect me to believe he came in here two or three times and you didn't find out who he was?"

"I didn't mean exactly I didn't know his name," Big Smiley hemmed. "But I'se telling you, Chief, ain't no leads 'round here, that's for sure."

"You're going to have to tell me more than that, son," Grave Digger said in a flat, toneless voice.

Big Smiley looked at him; then suddenly he leaned across the bar and said in a low voice, "Try at Bucky's, Chief."

"Why Bucky's?"

"I seen him come in here once with a pimp what hangs 'round in Bucky's."

"What's his name?"

"I don't recollect his name, Chief. They driv up in his car and just stopped for a minute like they was looking for somebody and went out and drive away."

"Don't play with me," Grave Digger said with a sudden show of anger. "This ain't the movies; this is real. A white man has been killed in Harlem and Harlem is my beat. I'll take you down to the station and turn a dozen white cops loose on you and they'll work you over until the black comes off."

"Name's Ready Belcher, Chief, but I don't want nobody to know I told you," Big Smiley said in a whisper. "I don't want no trouble with that starker."

"Ready," Grave Digger said and got down from his stool.

He didn't know much about Ready; just that he operated up-town on the swank side of Harlem, above 145th Street in Washington Heights.

He drove up to the 154th Street precinct station at the corner of Amsterdam Avenue and asked for his friend, Bill Cresus. Bill was a colored detective on the vice squad. No one knew where Bill was at the time. He left word for Bill to contact him at Bucky's if he called within the hour. Then he got into his car and coasted down the sharp incline to St. Nicholas Avenue and turned south down the lesser incline past 149th Street.

Outwardly it was a quiet neighbourhood of private houses and five- and six-story apartment buildings flanking the wide black-paved street. But the houses had been split up into bed-sized one-room kitchenettes, renting for $25 weekly, at the disposal of frantic couples who wished to shack up for a season. And behind the respectable-looking facades of the apartment buildings were the plush flesh cribs and poppy pads and circus tents of Harlem.

The excitement of the dragnet hadn't reached this far and the street was comparatively empty.

He coasted to a stop before a sedate basement entrance. Four steps below street level was a black door with a shiny brass knocker in the shape of three musical notes. Above it red neon lights spelled out the word *BUCKY'S*.

It felt strange to be alone. The last time had been when Coffin Ed was in the hospital after the acid throwing. The memory of it made his head tight with anger and it took a special effort to keep his temper under wraps.

He pushed and the door opened.

People sat at white-clothed tables beneath pink-shaded wall lights in a long narrow room, eating fried chicken daintily with their fingers. There was a white party of six, several colored couples, and two colored men with white women. They looked well-dressed and reasonably clean.

The walls behind them were covered with innumerable small pink-stained pencil portraits of all the great and the near-great who had ever lived in Harlem. Musicians led nine to one.

The hat-check girl stationed in a cubicle beside the entrance stuck out her hand with a supercilious look.

Grave Digger kept his hat on and strode down the narrow aisle between the tables.

A chubby pianist with shining black skin and a golden smile who was dressed in a tan tweed sport jacket and white silk sport shirt open at the throat sat at a baby grand piano wedged between the last table and the circular bar. Soft white light spilled on his partly bald head while he played nocturnes with a bedroom touch.

He gave Grave Digger an apprehensive look, got up and followed him to the semi-darkness of the bar.

"I hope you're not on business, Digger. I pay to keep this place off-limits for cops," he said in a fluttery voice.

Grave Digger's gaze circled the bar. Its high stools were inhabited by a varied crew: a big dark-haired white man, two slim young colored men, a short heavy-set white man with blond crew-cut hair, two dark women dressed in white silk evening gowns, a chocolate dandy in a box-backed double-breasted tuxedo sporting a shoestring dubonet bow. A high-yellow waitress waited nearby with a serving tray. Another tall, slim ebony young man presided over the bar.

"I'm just looking around, Bucky," Grave Digger said. "Just looking for a break."

"Many folks have found a break in here," Bucky said suggestively.

"I don't doubt it."

"But that's not the kind of break you're looking for."

"I'm looking for a break on a case. An important white man was shot to death over on Lenox Avenue a short time ago."

Bucky gestured with lotioned hands. His manicured nails flashed in the dim light. "What has that to do with us here? Nobody ever gets hurt in here. Everything is smooth and quiet. You can see for yourself. Genteel people dining in leisure. Fine food. Soft music. Low lights and laughter. Doesn't look like business for the police in this respectable atmosphere."

In the pause that followed, one of the marcelled ebonies was heard saying in a lilting voice, "I positively did not even look at her man, and she upped and knocked me over the head with a whisky bottle."

"These black bitches are so violent," his companion said.

"And strong, honey."

Grave Digger smiled sourly.

"The man who was killed was a patron of yours," he said. "Name of Ulysses Galen."

"My God, Digger, I don't know the names of all the ofays who come into my place," Bucky said. "I just play for them and try to make them happy."

"I believe you," Grave Digger said. "Galen was seen about town with Ready. Does that stir your memory?"

"Ready?" Bucky exclaimed innocently. "He hardly ever comes in here. Who gave you that notion?"

"The hell he doesn't," Grave Digger said. "He panders out of here."

"You hear that!" Bucky appealed to the barman in a shrill horrified voice, then caught himself as the silence from the diners reached his sensitive ears. With hushed indignation he added, "This flatfoot comes in here and accuses me of harboring panderers."

"A little bit of that goes a long way, son," Grave Digger said in his flat voice.

"Oh, that man's an ogre, Bucky," the barman said. "You go back to your entertaining and I'll see what he wants." He switched over to the bar, put his hands on his hips and looked down at Grave Digger with a haughty air. "And just what can we do for you, you mean rude grumpy man?"

The white men at the bar laughed.

Bucky turned and started off.

Grave Digger caught him by the arm and pulled him back. "Don't make me get rough, son," he muttered.

"Don't you dare manhandle me," Bucky said in a low tense whisper, his whole chubby body quivering with indignation. "I don't have to take that from you. I'm covered."

The bartender backed away, shaking himself. "Don't let him hurt Bucky," he appealed to the white men in a frightened voice.

"Maybe I can help you," the white man with the blond crew cut said to Grave Digger. "You're a detective, aren't you?"

"Yeah," Grave Digger said, holding on to Bucky. "A white man was killed in Harlem tonight and I'm looking for the killer."

The white man's eyebrows went up an inch.

"Do you expect to find him here?"

"I'm following a lead, is all. The man has been seen with a pimp called Ready Belcher who hangs out here."

The white man's eyebrows subsided.

"Oh, Ready; I know him. But he's merely –"

Bucky cut him off: "You don't have to tell him anything; you're protected in here."

"Sure," the white man said. "That's what the officer is trying to do, protect us all."

"He's right," one of the evening-gowned colored women said. "If Ready has killed some trick he was steering to Reba's the chair's too good for him."

"Shut your mouth, woman," the barman whispered fiercely.

The muscles in Grave Digger's face began to jump as he let go of Bucky. He stood up with his heels hooked into the rungs of the barstool and leaned over the bar. He caught the barman by the front of his red silk shirt as he was trying to dance away. The shirt ripped down the seam with a ragged sound but enough held for him to jerk the barman close to the bar.

"You got too goddamned much to say, Tarbelle," he said in a thick cottony voice, and slapped the barman spinning across the circular enclosure with the palm of his open hand.

"He didn't have to do that," the first woman said.

Grave Digger turned on her and said thickly, "And you, little sister, you and me are going to see Reba."

"Reba!" her companion replied. "Do I know anybody named Reba. Lord no!"

Grave Digger stepped down from his high stool.

"Cut that Aunt Jemima routine and get up off your ass," he said thickly, "or I'll take my pistol and break off your teeth."

The two white men stared at him as though at a dangerous animal escaped from the zoo.

"You mean that?" the woman said.

"I mean it," he said.

She scrunched out of the stool and said, "Gimme my coat, Jule."

The chocolate dandy took a coat from the top of the jukebox behind them.

"That's putting it on rather thick," the blond white man protested in a reasonable voice.

"I'm just a cop," Grave Digger said thickly. "If you white people insist on coming up to Harlem where you force colored people to live in vice-and-crime-ridden slums, it's my job to see that you are safe."

The white man turned bright red.

8

The sergeant knocked at the door. He was flanked by two uniformed cops and a corporal.

Another search party led by another sergeant was at the door across the hall.

Other cops were working all the corridors starting at the bottom and sealing off the area they'd covered.

"Come in," Granny called in a querulous voice. "The door ain't locked." She bit the stem of her corn-cob pipe with toothless gums.

The sergeant and his party entered the small kitchen. It was crowded.

At the sight of the very old woman working innocently at her darning, the sergeant started to remove his cap, then remembered he was on duty and kept it on.

"You don't lock your door, Grandma?" he observed.

Granny looked at the cops over the rims of her ancient spectacles and her old fingers went lax on the darning egg.

"Naw suh, Ah ain't got nuthin' for nobody to steal and ain't nobody want nuthin' else from an old 'oman like me."

The sergeant's beady blue eyes scanned the kitchen. "You keep this place mighty clean, Grandma," he remarked in surprise.

"Yes suh, it don't kill a body to keep clean and my old missy used to always say de cleaness is next to the goddess."

Her old milky eyes held a terrified question she couldn't ask and her thin old body began to tremble.

"You mean goodness," the sergeant said.

"Naw suh, Ah means goddess; Ah knows what she said."

"She means cleanliness is next to godliness," the corporal interposed.

"The professor," one of the cops said.

Granny pursed her lips. "Ah know what my missy said; goddess, she said."

"Were you in slavery?" the sergeant asked as though struck suddenly by the thought.

The others stared at her with sudden interest.

"Ah don't rightly know, suh. Ah 'spect so though."

"How old are you?"

Her lips moved soundlessly; she seemed to be trying to remember.

"She must be all of a hundred," the professor said.

She couldn't stop her body from trembling and slowly it got worse.

"What for you white 'licemen wants with me, suh?" she finally asked.

The sergeant noticed that she was trembling and said reassuringly, "We ain't after you, Grandma; we're looking for an escaped prisoner and some teenage gangsters."

"Gangsters!"

Her spectacles slipped down on her nose and her hands

shook as though she had the palsy.

"They belong to a neighbourhood gang that calls itself Real Cool Moslems."

She went from terrified to scandalized. "We ain't no heathen in here, suh," she said indignantly. "We be God-fearing Christians."

The cops laughed.

"They're not real Moslems," the sergeant said. "They just call themselves that. One of them, named Sonny Pickens, is older than the rest. He killed a white man outside on the street."

The darning dropped unnoticed from Granny's nerveless fingers. The corncob pipe wobbled in her puckered mouth; the professor looked at it with morbid fascination.

"A white man! Merciful hebens!" she exclaimed in a quavering voice. "What's this wicked world coming to?"

"Nobody knows," the sergeant said, then changed his manner abruptly. "Well, let's get down to business, Grandma. What's your name?"

"Bowee, suh, but e'body calls me Granny."

"Bowee. How do you spell that, Grandma?"

"Ah don't rightly know, suh. Hit's just short for boll weevil. My old missy name me that. They say the boll weevil was mighty bad the year Ah was born."

"What about your husband, didn't he have a name?"

"Ah neber had no regular 'usban', suh. Just whosoever was thar."

"You got any children?"

"Jesus Christ, sarge," the professor said. "Her youngest child would be sixty years old."

The two cops laughed; the sergeant reddened sheepishly.

"Who lives here with you, Granny?" the sergeant continued.

Her bony frame stiffened beneath her faded Mother Hubbard. The corncob pipe fell into her lap and rolled unnoticed to the floor.

"Just me and mah grandchile, Caleb, suh," she said in a

forced voice. "And Ah rents a room to two workin' boys; but they be good boys and don't neber bother nobody."

The cops grew suddenly speculative.

"Now this grandchild, Caleb, Grandma –" the sergeant began cunningly.

"He might be mah great-grandchile, suh," she interrupted.

He frowned, "Great, then. Where is he now?"

"You mean right now, suh?"

"Yeah, Grandma, right this minute."

"He at work in a bowling alley downtown, suh."

"How long has he been at work?"

"He left right after supper, suh. We gennally eats supper at six o'clock."

"And he has a regular job in this bowling alley?"

"Naw suh, hit's just for t'night, suh. He goes to school – Ah don't rightly 'member the number of his new P.S."

"Where is this bowling alley he's working at tonight?"

"Ah don't know, suh. Ah guess you all'll have to ast Samson. He is one of mah roomers."

"Samson, yeah." The sergeant stored it in his memory. "And you haven't seen Caleb since supper – about seven o'clock, say?"

"Ah don't know what time it was but it war right after supper."

"And when he left here he went directly to work?"

"Yas suh, you find him right dar on de job. He a good boy and always mind me what Ah say."

"And your roomers, where are they?"

"They is in they room, suh. Hit's in the front. They got visitors with 'em."

"Visitors?"

"Gals."

"Oh!" Then to his assistants he said, "Come on."

They went through the middle room like hounds on a hot scent. The sergeant tried the handle to the front-room door without knocking, found it locked and hammered angrily.

"Who's that?" Sheik asked.

"The police."

Sheik unlocked the door. The cops rushed in. Sheik's eyes glittered.

"What the hell do you keep your door locked for?" the sergeant asked.

"We didn't want to be disturbed."

Four pairs of eyes quickly scanned the room.

Two teenaged colored girls sat side by side on the bed, leafing through a colored picture magazine. Another youth stood looking out the open window at the excitement on the street.

"Who the hell you think you're kidding with this phony stage setting?" the sergeant roared.

"Not you, ace," Sheik said flippantly.

The sergeant's hand flicked out like a whip, passing inches in front of Sheik's eyes.

Sheik jumped back as though he'd been scalded.

"Jagged to the gills," the sergeant said, looking minutely about the room. His eyes lit on Choo-Choo's half-smoked package of Camels on the table. "Dump out those fags," he ordered a cop, watching Sheik's reaction. "Never mind," he added. "The bastard's got rid of them."

He closed in on Sheik like a prizefighter and shoved his red sweaty face within a few inches of Sheik's. His veined blue eyes bored into Sheik's pale yellow eyes.

"Where's that A-rab costume?" he asked in a browbeating voice.

"What Arab costume? Do I look like an A-rab to you?"

"You look like a two-bit punk to me. You got the eyes of a yellow cur."

"You ain't got no prize-winning eyes yourself."

"Don't give me none of your lip, punk; I'll knock out your teeth."

"I could knock out your teeth too if I had on a sergeant's uniform and three big flatfeet backing me up."

The cops stared at him from blank shuttered faces.

"What do they call you, Mo-hammed or Nasser?" the sergeant hammered.

"They call me by my name, Samson."

"Samson what?"

"Samson Hyers."

"Don't give me that crap; we know you're one of those Moslems."

"I ain't no Moslem; I'm a cannibal."

"Oh, so you think you're a comedian."

"You the one asking the funny questions."

"What's that other punk's name?"

"Ask him."

The sergeant slapped him with such force it sounded like a .22-caliber shot.

Sheik reeled back from the impact of the slap but kept his feet. Blood darkened his face to the color of beef liver; the imprint of the sergeant's hand glowed purple red. His pale yellow eyes looked wildcat crazy. But he kept his lip buttoned.

"When I ask you a question I want you to answer it," the sergeant said.

He didn't answer.

"You hear me?"

He still didn't answer.

The sergeant loomed in front of him with both fists cocked like red meat axes.

"I want an answer."

"Yeah, I hear you," Sheik muttered sullenly.

"Frisk him," the sergeant ordered the professor, then to the other two cops; said, "You and Price start shaking down this room."

The professor set to work on Sheik methodically, as though searching for lice, while the other cops started dumping dresser drawers onto the table.

The sergeant left them and turned his attention to Choo-Choo.

"What kind of Moslem are you?"

Choo-Choo started grinning and fawning like the original Uncle Tom.

"I ain't no Moslem, boss, I'se just a plain old unholy roller."

"I guess your name is Delilah."

"He-he, naw suh boss, but you're warm. It's Justice Broome."

All three cops looked about and grinned, and the sergeant had to clamp his jaws to keep from grinning too.

"You know these Moslems?"

"What Moslems, boss?"

"The Harlem Moslems in this neighbourhood."

"Naw suh, boss, I don't know no Moslems in Harlem."

"You think I was born yesterday? They a neighbourhood gang. Every black son of a bitch in this neighbourhood knows who they are."

"Everybody 'cept me, boss."

The sergeant's palm flew out and caught Choo-Choo unexpectedly on the mouth while it was still open in a grin. It didn't rock his short thick body, but his eyes rolled back in their sockets. He spit blood on the floor.

"Boss, suh, please be careful with my chops – they're tender."

"I'm getting damn tired of your lying."

"Boss, I swear 'fore God, if I knowed anything 'bout them Moslems you'd be the first one I'd tell it to."

"What do you do?"

"I works, boss, yes suh."

"Doing what?"

"I helps out."

"Helps out with what? You want to lose some of your pearly teeth?"

"I helps out a man who writes numbers."

"What's his name?"

"His name?"

The sergeant cocked his fists.

"Oh, you mean his name, boss. Hit's Four-Four Row."

"You call that a name?"
"Yas suh, that's what they calls him."
"What does your buddy do?"
"The same thing," Sheik said.
The sergeant wheeled on him. "You keep quiet; when I want you I'll call you." Then he said to the professor, "Can't you keep that punk quiet?"
The professor unhooked his sap. "I'll quiet him."
"I don't want you to quiet him; just keep him quiet. I got some more questions for him." Then he turned back to Choo-Choo. "When do you punks work?"
"In the morning, boss. We got to get the numbers in by noon."
"What do you do the rest of the day?"
"Go 'round and pay off."
"What if there isn't any payoff?"
"Just go 'round."
"Where's your beat?"
" 'Round here."
"God damn it, you mean to tell me you write numbers in this neighbourhood and you don't know anything about the Moslems?"
"I swear on my mother's grave, boss, I ain't never heard of no Moslems 'round here. They must not be in this neighbourhood, boss."
"What time did you leave the house tonight?"
"I ain't never left it, boss. We come here right after we et supper and ain't been out since."
"Stop lying; I saw you both when you slipped back in here a half-hour ago."
"Naw suh, boss, you musta seen somebody what looks like us 'cause we been here all the time."
The sergeant crossed to the door and flung it open. "Hey, Grandma!" he called.
"Hannh?" she answered querulously from the kitchen.
"How long have these boys been in their room?"
"Hannh?"

"You have to talk louder; she can't hear you," Sissie volunteered.

Sheik and Choo-Choo gave her threatening looks.

The sergeant crossed the middle room to the kitchen door. "How long have your roomers been back from supper?" he roared.

She looked at him from uncomprehending eyes.

"Hannh?"

"She can't hear no more," Sissie called. "She gets that way sometime."

"Hell," the sergeant said disgustedly and stormed back to Choo-Choo. "Where'd you pick up these girls?"

"We didn't pick 'em up, boss; they come here by themselves."

"You're too goddam innocent to be alive." The sergeant was frustrated. He turned to the professor: "What did you find on that punk?"

"This knife."

"Hell," the sergeant said. He took it and dropped it into his pocket without a glance. "Okay, fan this other punk – Justice."

"I'll do Justice," the professor punned.

The two cops crossed glances suggestively.

They had dumped out all the drawers and turned out all the boxes and pasteboard suitcases and now they were ready for the bed.

"You gals rise and shine," one said.

The girls got up and stood uncomfortably in the center of the room.

"Find anything?" the sergeant asked.

"Nothing that I'd even care to have in my dog house," the cop said.

The sergeant began on the girls. "What's your name?" he asked Sissie.

"Sissieratta Hamilton."

"Sissie what?"

"Sissieratta."

"Where do you live, Sissie?"

"At 2702 Seventh Avenue with my aunt and uncle, Mr. and Mrs. Coolie Dunbar."

"Ummm," he said, "And yours?" he asked Sugartit.

"Evelyn Johnson."

"Where do you live, Eve?"

"In Jamaica with my parents, Mr. and Mrs. Edward Johnson."

"It's mighty late for you to be so far from home."

"I'm going to spend the night with Sissieratta."

"How long have you girls been here?" he asked of both.

"About half an hour, more or less," Sissie replied.

"Then you saw the shooting down on the street?"

"It was over when we got here."

"Where did you come from?"

"From my house."

"You don't know if these punks have been in all evening or not."

"They were here when we got here and they said they'd been waiting here since supper. We promised to come at eight but we had to stay help my aunty and we got here late."

"Sounds too good to be true," the sergeant commented.

The girls didn't reply.

The cops finished with the bed and the talkative one said, "Nothing but stink."

"Can that talk," the sergeant said. "Grandma's clean."

"These punks aren't."

The sergeant turned to the professor. "What's on Justice besides the blindfold?"

His joke laid an egg.

"Nothing but his black," the professor said.

His joke drew a laugh.

"What do you say, shall we run 'em in?" the sergeant asked.

"Why not," the professor said. "If we haven't got space in the bullpen for everybody we can put up tents."

The sergeant wheeled suddenly on Sheik as though he'd forgotten something.

"Where's Caleb?"

"Up on the roof tending his pigeons."

All four cops froze. They stared at Sheik with those blank shuttered looks.

Finally the sergeant said carefully, "His grandma said you told her he was working in a bowling alley downtown."

"We just told her that to keep her from worrying. She don't like for him to go up on the roof at night."

"If I find you punks are holding out on me, God help you," the sergeant said in a slow sincere voice.

"Go look then," Sheik said.

The sergeant nodded to the professor. The professor climbed out of the window into the bright glare of the spotlights and began ascending the fire escape.

"What's he doing with them at night?" the sergeant asked Sheik.

"I don't know. Trying to make them lay black eggs, I suppose."

"I'm going to take you down to the station and have a private talk with you, punk," the sergeant said. "You're one punk who needs talking to privately."

The professor came down from the roof and called through the window, "They're holding two coons up here beside a pigeon loft. They're waiting on you."

"Okay, I'm coming. You and Price hold these punks on ice," he directed the other cops and climbed out of the window behind the professor.

9

"Get in," Grave Digger said.

She pulled up the skirt of her evening gown, drew the black coat tight, and eased her jumbo hams into the seat usually occupied by Coffin Ed.

Grave Digger went around on the other side and climbed beneath the wheel and waited.

"Does I just have to go along, honey," the woman said in a wheedling voice. "I can just as well tell you where she's at."

"That's what I'm waiting for."

"Well, why didn't you say so? She's in the Knickerbocker Apartments on 45th Street – the old Knickerbocker, I mean. She on the six story, 669."

"Who is she?" Grave Digger asked, probing a little.

"Who she is? Just a landprop is all."

"That ain't what I mean."

"Oh, I know what you means. You means who is she. You means you don't know who Reba is, Digger?" She tried to sound jocular but wasn't successful. "She the landprop what used to be old cap Murphy's go-between 'fore he got sent up for taking all them bribes. It was in all the papers."

"That was ten years ago and they called her Sheba then," he said.

"Yare, that's right, but she changed her name after she got into that last shooting scrape. You musta 'member that. She caught the nigger with some chippie or 'nother and made him jump buck naked out the third-story window. That wouldn't 'ave been so bad but she shot 'im through the head as he was going down. That was when she lived in the valley. Since then she done come up here on the hill. 'Course it warn't nobody but her husband and she didn't get a day. But

Reba always has been lucky that way."

He took a shot in the dark. "What would anybody shoot Galen for?"

She grew stiff with caution, "Who he?"

"You know damn well who he was. He's the man who was shot tonight."

"Naw suh, I didn't know nothing 'bout that gennelman. I don't know why nobody would want to shoot him."

"You people give me a pain in the seat with all that ducking and dodging every time someone asks you a question. You act like you belong to a race of artful dodgers."

"You is asking me something I don't know nothing 'bout."

"Okay, get out."

She got out faster than she got in.

He drove down the hill of St. Nicholas Avenue and turned up the hill of 145th Street toward Convent Avenue.

On the left-hand corner, next to a new fourteen-story apartment building erected by a white insurance company, was the Brown Bomber Bar; across from it Big Crip's Bar; on the right-hand corner Cohen's Drug Store with its iron-grilled windows crammed with electric hair straightening irons, Hi-Life hair cream, Black and White bleaching cream, SSS and 666 blood tonics, Dr. Scholl's corn pads, men's and women's nylon head caps with chin straps to press hair while sleeping, a bowl of blue stone good for body lice, tins of Sterno canned heat good for burning or drinking, Halloween postcards and all the latest in enamelware hygiene utensils; across from it Zazully's Delicatessen with a white-lettered announcement on the plate-glass window: *We Have Frozen Chitterlings and Other Hard-to-find Delicacies.*

Grave Digger parked in front of a big frame house with peeling yellow paint which had been converted into offices, got out and walked next door to a six-story rotten-brick tenement long overdue at the wreckers.

Three cars were parked at the curb in front; two with

upstate New York plates and the other from mid-Manhattan.

He pushed open a scaly door beneath the arch of a concrete block on which the word *KNICKER-BOCKER* was embossed.

An old gray-haired man with a splotched brown face sat in a chair just inside the doorway to the semi-dark corridor. He cautiously drew back gnarled feet in felt bedroom slippers and looked Grave Digger over with dull, satiated eyes.

"Evenin'," he said.

Grave Digger glanced at him. "Evenin'."

"Fourth story on de right. Number 421," the old man informed him.

Grave Digger stopped. "That Reba's?"

"You don't want Reba's. You want Topsy's. Dat's 421."

"What's happening at Topsy's?"

"What always happen. Dat's where the trouble is."

"What kind of trouble?"

"Just general trouble. Fightin' and cuttin'."

"I'm not looking for trouble. I'm looking for Reba."

"You're the man, ain't you?"

"Yeah, I'm the man."

"Then you wants 421. I'se de janitor."

"If you're the janitor then you know Mr. Galen."

A veil fell over the old man's face. "Who he?"

"He's the big Greek man who goes up to Reba's."

"I don't know no Greeks, boss. Don't no white folks come in here. Nothin' but cullud folks. You'll find 'em all at Topsy's."

"He was killed over on Lenox tonight."

"Sho nuff?"

Grave Digger started off.

The old man called to him, "I guess you wonderin' why we got them big numbers on de doors."

Grave Digger paused. "All right, why?"

"They sounds good." The old man cackled.

Grave Digger walked up five flights of shaky wooden stairs and knocked on a red-painted door with a round glass peephole in the upper panel.

After an interval a heavy woman's voice asked, "Who's you?"

"I'm the Digger."

Bolts clicked and the door cracked a few inches on the chain. A big dark silhouette loomed in the crack, outlined by blue light from behind.

"I didn't recognize you, Digger," a pleasant bass voice said. "Your hat shades your face. Long time no see."

"Unchain the door, Reba, before I shoot it off."

A deep bass laugh accompanied chain rattling and the door swung inward.

"Same old Digger, shoot first and talk later. Come on in; we're all colored folks here."

He stepped into a blue-lit carpeted hall reeking of incense.

"You're sure?"

She laughed again as she closed and bolted the door. "Those are not folks, those are clients." Then she turned casually to face him. "What's on your mind, honey?"

She was as tall as his six feet two, with snow-white hair cut short as a man's and brushed straight back from her forehead. Her lips were painted carnation red and her eyelids silver but her smooth unlined jet black skin was untouched. She wore a black sequined evening gown with a red rose in the V of her mammoth bosom, which was a lighter brown than her face. She looked like the last of the Amazons blackened by time.

"Where can we talk?" Grave Digger said. "I don't want to strain you."

"You don't strain me, honey," she said, opening the first door to the right. "Come into the kitchen."

She put a bottle of bourbon and a siphon beside two tall glasses on the table and sat in a kitchen chair.

"Say when," she said as she started to pour.

"By me," Grave Digger said, pushing his hat to the back

of his head and planting a foot on the adjoining chair.

She stopped pouring and put down the bottle.

"You go ahead," he said.

"I don't drink no more," she said. "I quit after I killed Sam."

He crossed his arms on his raised knee and leaned forward on them, looking at her.

"You used to wear a rosary," he said.

She smiled, showing gold crowns on her outside incisors.

"When I got real religion I quit that too," she said.

"What religion did you get?"

"Just the faith, Digger, just the spirit."

"It lets you run this joint?"

"Why not. It's nature, just like eating. Nothing in my faith 'gainst eating. I just make it convenient and charge 'em for it."

"You'd better get a new steerer; the one downstairs is simple-minded."

Her big bass laugh rang out again. "He don't work for us; he does that on his own."

"Don't make it hard on yourself," he said. "This can be easy for us both."

She looked at him calmly. "I ain't got nothing to fear."

"When was the last time you saw Galen?"

"The big Greek? Been some time now, Digger. Three or four months. He don't come here no more."

"Why?"

"I don't let him."

"How come?"

"Be your age, Digger. This is a sporting house. If I don't let a white john with money come here, I must have good reasons. And if I want to keep my other white clients I'd better not say what they are. You can't close me up and you can't make me talk, so why don't you let it go at that?"

"The Greek was shot to death tonight over on Lenox."

"I just heard it over the radio," she said.

"I'm trying to find out who did it."

She looked at him in surprise. "It said on the radio the killer was known. A Sonny Pickens. Said a teenage gang called the something-or-'nother Moslems snatched him."

"He didn't do it. That's why I'm here."

"Well, if he didn't do it, you got your job cut out," she said. "I wish I could help you but I can't."

"Maybe," he said. "Maybe not."

She raised her eyebrows slightly. "By the way, where's your sidekick, Coffin Ed? The radio said he shot one of the gang."

"Yeah, he got suspended."

She became still, like an animal alert to danger. "Don't take it out on me, Digger."

"I just want to know why you stopped the Greek from coming here."

She stared into his eyes. She had dark brown eyes with clear whites and long black lashes.

"I'll let you talk to Ready. He knows."

"Is he here now?"

"He got a little chippie here he can't stay 'way from for five minutes. I'm going to throw 'em both out soon. Would have before now but my clients like her."

"Was the Greek her client?"

She got up slowly, sighing slightly from the effort.

"I'll send him out here."

"Bring him out."

"All right. But take him away, Digger. I don't want him talking in here. I don't want no more trouble. I've had trouble all my days."

"I'll take him away," he said.

She went out and Grave Digger heard doors being discreetly opened and shut and then her controlled bass voice saying, "How do I know? He said he was a friend."

A tall man with pockmarked skin a dirty shade of black stepped into the kitchen. An old razor scar cut a purple ridge from the lobe of his ear to the tip of his chin. There was a cast in one eye, the other was reddish brown. Thin corked hair stuck to a double-jointed head shaped like a peanut. He was flashily dressed in a light tan suit. Glass glittered from two gold-plated rings. His pointed tan shoes were shined to mirror brilliance.

At sight of Grave Digger he drew up short and turned a murderous look on Reba.

"You tole me hit was a friend," he accused in a rough voice.

She didn't let it bother her. She pushed him into the kitchen and closed the door.

"Well, ain't he?" she asked.

"What's this, some kind of frame-up?" he shouted.

Grave Digger chuckled at the look of outrage on his face. "How can a buck as ugly as you be a pimp?" he asked.

"You're gonna make me talk about you mamma," Ready said, digging his right hand into his pants pocket.

With nothing moving but his arm, Grave Digger backhanded him in the solar plexus, knocking out his wind, then pivoted on his left foot and followed with a right cross to the same spot, and with the same motion raised his knee and sunk it into Ready's belly as the pimp's slim frame jackknifed forward. Spit showered from Ready's fishlike mouth, and the sense was already gone from his eyes when Grave Digger grabbed him by the back of the coat collar, jerked him erect, and started to slap him in the face with his open palm.

Reba grabbed his arm, saying. "Not in here, Digger, I beg you; don't make him bleed. You said you'd take him out."

"I'm taking him out now," he said in a cottony voice, shaking off her hold.

"Then finish him without bleeding him; I don't want nobody coming in here finding blood on the floor."

Grave Digger grunted and eased off. He propped Ready against the wall, holding him up on his rubbery legs with one hand while he took the knife and frisked him quickly with the other.

The sense came back into Ready's good eye and Grave

Digger stepped back and said, "All right, let's go quietly, son."

Ready fussed about without looking at him, straightening his coat and tie, then fished a greasy comb from his pocket and combed his rumpled conk. He was bent over in the middle from pain and breathing in gasps. A white froth had collected in both corners of his mouth.

Finally he mumbled, "You can't take me outa here without no warrant."

"Go ahead with the man and shut up," Reba said quickly.

He gave her a pleading look. "You gonna let him take me outa here?"

"If he don't I'm going to throw you out myself," she said. "I don't want any hollering and screaming in here scaring my white clients."

"That's gonna cost you," Ready threatened.

"Don't threaten me, nigger," she said dangerously. "And don't set your foot in my door again."

"Okay, Reba, that's the lick that killed Dick," Ready said slowly. "You and him got me outnumbered." He gave her a last sullen look and turned to go.

Reba walked to the door and let them out.

"I hope I get what I want," Grave Digger said. "If I don't I'll be back."

"If you don't it's your own fault," she said.

He marched Ready ahead of him down the shaky stairs.

The old man in the ragged red chair looked up in surprise.

"You got the wrong nigger," he said. "Hit ain't him what's makin' all the trouble."

"Who is it?" Grave Digger asked.

"Hit's Cocky. He the one what's always pulling his shiv."

Grave Digger filed the information for future reference.

"I'll keep this one since he's the one I've got," he said.

"Balls," the old man said disgustedly. "He's just a halfass pimp."

10

White light coming from the street slanted upward past the edge of the roof and made a milky wall in the dark.

Beyond the wall of light the flat tar roof was shrouded in semi-darkness.

The sergeant emerged from the edge of light like a hammerhead turtle rising from the deep. In one glance he saw Sonny frantically beating a flock of panic-stricken pigeons with a long bamboo pole, and Inky standing motionless as though he'd sprouted from the tar.

"By God, now I know why they're called tarbabies!" he exclaimed.

Gripping the pole for dear life with both gauntleted hands, Sonny speared desperately at the pigeons. His eyes were white as they rolled toward the red-faced sergeant. His ragged overcoat flapped in the wind. The pigeons ducked and dodged and flew in lopsided circles. Their heads were cocked on one side as they observed Sonny's gymnastics with beady apprehension.

Inky stood like a silhouette cut from black paper, looking at nothing. The whites of his eyes gleamed in the dark.

The pigeon loft was a rickety coop about six feet high, made of scraps of chicken wire, discarded screen windows and assorted rags tacked to a frame of rotten boards propped against the low brick wall separating the roofs. It had a tarpaulin top and was equipped with precarious roosts, tin cans of rusty water, and a rusty tin feeding pan.

Blue-uniformed white cops formed a jagged semi-circle in front of it, staring at Sonny in silent and bemused amazement.

The sergeant climbed onto the roof, puffing, and paused for a moment to mop his brow.

"What's he doing, voodoo?" he asked.

"It's only Don Quixote in blackface dueling a windmill," the professor said.

"That ain't funny," the sergeant said. "I like Don Quixote."

The professor let it go.

"Is he a halfwit?" the sergeant said.

"If he's got that much," the professor said.

The sergeant pushed to the center of the stage, but once there hesitated as though he didn't know how to begin.

Sonny looked at him through the corners of his eyes and kept working the pole. Inky stared at nothing with silent intensity.

"All right, all right, so your feet don't stink," the sergeant said. "Which one of you is Caleb?"

"Dass me," Sonny said, without an instant neglecting the pigeons.

"What the hell you call yourself doing?"

"I'se teaching my pigeons how to fly."

The sergeant's jowls began to swell. "You trying to be funny?"

"Naw suh, I didn' mean they didn' know how to fly. They can fly all right at day but they don't know how to night fly."

The sergeant looked at the professor. "Don't pigeons fly at night?"

"Search me," the professor said.

"Naw suh, not unless you makes 'em," Inky said.

Everybody looked at him.

"Hell, he can talk," the professor said.

"They sleeps," Sonny added.

"Roosts," Inky corrected.

"We're going to make some pigeons fly, too," the sergeant said. "Stool pigeons."

"If they don't fly, they'll fry," the professor said.

The sergeant turned to Inky. "What do they call you, boy?"

"Inky," Inky said. "But my name's Rufus Tree."
"So you're Inky," the sergeant said.
"They're both Inky," the professor said.
The cops laughed.
The sergeant smiled into his hand. Then he wheeled abruptly on Sonny and shouted, "Sonny! Drop that pole!"
Sonny gave a violent start and speared a pigeon in the craw, but he hung on to the pole. The pigeon flew crazily into the light and kept on going. Sonny watched it until he got control of himself, then he turned slowly and looked at the sergeant with big innocent white eyes.
"You talking to me, boss?" His black face shone with sweat.
"Yeah, I'm talking to you, Sonny."
"They don't calls me, Sonny, boss; they calls me Cal."
"You look like a boy called Sonny."
"Lots of folks is called Sonny, boss."
"What did you jump for if your name isn't Sonny? You jumped halfway out of your skin."
"Most anybody'd jump with you hollerin' at 'em like that, boss."
The sergeant wiped off another smile. "You told your grandma you were going downtown to work."
"She don't want me messin' 'round these pigeons at night. She thinks I might fall off'n the roof."
"Where have you been since supper?"
"Right up here, boss."
"He's just been up here about a half an hour," one of the cops volunteered.
"Naw suh, I been here all the time," Sonny contradicted. "I been inside the coop."
"Ain't nobody in heah but us pigeons, boss," the professor cracked.
"Did you look in the coop?" the sergeant asked the cop.
The cop reddened. "No, I didn't; I wasn't looking for a screwball."
The sergeant glanced at the coop. "By God, boy, your

pigeons lead a hard life," he said. Then turning suddenly to the other cops, he asked, "Have these punks been frisked?"

"We were waiting for you," another cop replied.

The sergeant sighed theatrically. "Well, who are you waiting for now?"

Two cops converged on Inky with alacrity; the professor and a third cop took on Sonny.

"Put that damn pole down!" the sergeant shouted at Sonny.

"No, let him hold it," the professor said. "It keeps his hands up."

"What the hell are you wearing that heavy overcoat for?" The sergeant kept on picking at Sonny. He was frustrated.

"I'se cold," Sonny said. Sweat was running down his face in rivers.

"You look it," the sergeant said.

"Jesus Christ, this coat stinks," the professor complained, working Sonny over fast to get away from it.

"Nothing?" the sergeant asked when he'd finished.

"Nothing," the professor said. In his haste he hadn't thought to make Sonny put down the pole and take off his gauntlets.

The sergeant looked at the cops frisking Inky. They shook their heads.

"What's Harlem coming to?" the sergeant complained. "All right, you punks, get downstairs," the sergeant ordered.

"I got to get my pigeons in," Sonny said.

The sergeant looked at him.

Sonny leaned the pole against the coop and began moving. Inky opened the door of the coop and began moving too. The pigeons took one look at the open door and began rushing to get inside.

"IRT subway at Times Square," the professor remarked.

The cops laughed and moved on to the next roof.

The sergeant and the professor followed Inky and Sonny through the window and into the room below.

Sissie and Sugartit sat side by side on the bed again. Choo-Choo sat in the straight-backed chair. Sheik stood in the center of the floor with his feet wide apart, looking defiant. The two cops stood with their buttocks propped against the edge of the table, looking bored.

With the addition of the four others, the room was crowded.

Everybody looked at the sergeant, waiting his next move.

"Get Grandma in here," he said.

The professor went after her.

They heard him saying, "Grandma, you're needed."

There was no reply.

"Grandma!" they heard him shout.

"She's asleep," Sissie called to him. "She's hard to wake once she gets to sleep."

"She's not asleep," the professor called back in an angry tone of voice.

"All right, let her alone," the sergeant said.

The professor returned, red-faced with vexation. "She sat there looking at me without saying a word," he said.

"She gets like that," Sissie said. "She just sort of shuts out the world and quits seeing and hearing anything."

"No wonder her grandson's a halfwit," the professor said, giving Sonny a malicious look.

"Well, what the hell are we going to do with them?" the sergeant said in a frustrated tone of voice.

The cops had no suggestions.

"Let's run them all in," the professor said.

The sergeant looked at him reflectively. "If we take in all the punks who look like them in this block, we'll have a thousand prisoners," he said.

"So what," the professor said. "We can't afford to risk losing Pickens because of a few hundred shines."

"Well, maybe we'd better," the sergeant said.

"Are you going to take her in too?" Sheik said, nodding toward Sugartit on the bed. "She's Coffin Ed's daughter."

The sergeant wheeled on him. "What! What's that about

Coffin Ed?"

"Evelyn Johnson there is his daughter," Sheik said evenly.

The cops turned as though their heads were synchronized and stared at her. No one spoke.

"Ask her," Sheik said.

The sergeant's face turned bright red.

It was the professor who spoke. "Well, girl? Are you Detective Johnson's daughter?"

Sugartit hesitated.

"Go on and tell 'em," Sheik said.

The red started crawling up the back of the sergeant's neck and engulfed his ears. "I don't like you," he said to Sheik, his voice constricted.

Sheik threw him a careless look, started to say something, then bit it off.

"Yes, I am," Sugartit said finally.

"We can soon check on that," the professor said, moving toward the window. "He and his partner must be in the vicinity."

"No, Jones might be, but Johnson was sent home," the sergeant said.

"What! Suspended?" the professor asked in surprise.

Sugartit looked startled; Sheik grinned smugly; the others remained impassive.

"Yeah, for killing the Moslem punk."

"For that?" the professor exclaimed indignantly. "Since when did they start penalizing policemen for shooting in self-defense?"

"I don't blame the chief," the sergeant said. "He's protecting himself. The punk was under-age and the newpapers are sure to put up a squawk."

"Anyway, Jones ought to know her," the professor said, going out on the fire escape and shouting to the cops below.

He couldn't make himself understood so he started down.

The sergeant asked Sugartit, "Have you got any identification?"

She drew a red leather card case from her skirt pocket and

handed it to him without speaking.

It held a black, white-lettered identification card with her photograph and thumbprint, similar to the one issued to policemen. It had been given to her as a souvenir for her sixteenth birthday and was signed by the chief of police.

The sergeant studied it for a moment and handed it back. He had seen others like it, his own daughter had one.

"Does your father know you're here visiting these hoodlums?" he asked.

"Certainly," Sugartit said. "They're friends of mine."

"You're lying," the sergeant said wearily.

"He doesn't know she's over here," Sissie put in.

"I know damn well he doesn't," the sergeant said.

"She's supposed to be visiting me."

"Well, do your folks know you're here?"

She dropped her gaze. "No."

"Eve and I are engaged," Sheik said with a smirk.

The sergeant wheeled toward him with his right cocked high. Sheik ducked automatically, his guard coming up. The sergeant hooked a left to his stomach underneath his guard, and when Sheik's guard dropped, he crossed his right to the side of Sheik's head, knocking him into a spinning stagger. Then he kicked him in the side of the stomach as he spun and, when he doubled over, the sergeant chopped him across the back of the neck with the meaty edge of his right hand. Sheik shuddered as though poleaxed and crashed to the floor. The sergeant took dead aim and kicked him in the valley of the buttocks with all his force.

The professor returned just in time to see the sergeant spit on him.

"Hey, what's happened to him?" he asked, climbing hastily through the window.

The sergeant took off his hat and wiped his perspiring forehead with a soiled white handkerchief. "His mouth did it," he said.

Sheik was groaning feebly, although unconscious.

The professor chuckled. "He's still trying to talk." Then

he said, "They couldn't find Jones. Lieutenant Anderson says he's working on another angle."

"It's okay, she's got an ID card," the sergeant said. Then asked, "Is the chief still there?"

"Yeah, he's still hanging around."

"Well, that's his job."

The professor looked about at the silent group. "What's the verdict?"

"Let's get on to the next house," the sergeant said. "If I'm here when this punk comes to I'll probably be the next one to get suspended."

"Can we leave the building now?" Sissie asked.

"You two girls can come with us," the sergeant offered.

Sheik groaned and rolled over.

"We can't leave him like that," she said.

The sergeant shrugged. The cops passed into the next room. The sergeant started to follow, then hesitated.

"All right, I'll fix it," he said.

He took the girls out on the fire escape and got the attention of the cops guarding the entrance below.

"Let these two girls pass!" he shouted.

The cops looked at the girls standing in the spotlight glare.

"Okay."

The sergeant followed them back into the room.

"If I were you I'd get the hell away from this punk fast," he advised, prodding Sheik with his toe. "He's headed straight for trouble, big trouble."

Neither replied.

He followed the professor out of the flat.

Granny sat unmoving in the rocking chair where they'd left her, tightly gripping the arms. She stared at them with an expression of fierce disapproval on her puckered old face and in her dim milky eyes.

"It's our job, Grandma," the sergeant said apologetically.

She didn't reply.

They passed on sheepishly.

Back in the front room, Sheik groaned and sat up.

Everyone moved at once. The girls moved away from him. Sonny began taking off the heavy overcoat. Inky and Choo-Choo bent over Sheik and, each taking an arm, began helping him to his feet.

"How you feel, Sheik?" Choo-Choo asked.

Sheik looked dazed. "Can't no copper hurt me," he muttered thickly, wobbling on his legs.

"Does it hurt?"

"Naw, it don't hurt," he said with a grimace of pain. Then he looked about stupidly. "They gone?"

"Yeah," Choo-Choo said jubilantly and cut a jig step. "We done beat 'em, Sheik. We done fooled 'em two ways sides and flat."

Sheik's confidence came back in a rush. "I told you we was going to do it."

Sonny grinned and raised his clasped hands in the prize-fight salute. "They had me sweating in the crotch," he confessed.

A look of crazed triumph distorted Sheik's flat, freckled face. "I'm the Sheik, Jack," he said. His yellow eyes were getting wild again.

Sissie looked at him and said apprehensively, "Me and Sugartit got to go. We were just waiting to see if you were all right."

"You can't go now – we got to celebrate," Sheik said.

"We ain't got nothing to celebrate with," Choo-Choo said.

"The hell we ain't," Sheik said. "Cops ain't so smart. You go up on the roof and get the pole."

"Who, me, Sheik?"

"Sonny then."

"Me!" Sonny said. "I done got enough of that roof."

"Go on," Sheik said. "You're a Moslem now and I command you in the name of Allah."

"Praise Allah," Choo-Choo said.

"I don't want to be no Moslem," Sonny said.

"All right, you're still our captive then," Sheik decreed. "You go get the pole, Inky. I got five sticks stashed in the end."

"Hell, I'll go," Choo-Choo said.

"No, let Inky go, he's been up there before and they won't think it's funny."

When Inky left for the pole, Sheik said to Choo-Choo, "Our captive's getting biggety since we saved him from the cops."

"I ain't gettin' biggety," Sonny declared. "I just want to get the hell outen here and get these cuffs off'n me without havin' to become no Moslem."

"You know too much for us to let you go now," Sheik said, exchanging a look with Choo-Choo.

Inky returned with the pole and, pulling the plug out of the end joint, he shook five cigarettes onto the table top.

"A feast!" Choo-Choo exclaimed. He grabbed one, opened the end with his thumb, and lit up.

Sheik lit another.

"Take one, Inky," he said.

Inky took one.

Everybody put on smoked glasses.

"Granny will smell it if you smoke in here," Sissie said.

"She thinks they're cubebs." Choo-Choo mimicked Granny: "Ah wish you chillens would stop smokin' them coo-bebs 'cause they make a body feel moughty funny in de head."

He and Sheik doubled over with laughter.

The room stank with the pungent smoke.

Sugartit picked up a stick, sat on the bed and lit it.

"Come on, baby, strip," Sheik urged her. "Celebrate your old man's flop by getting up off of some of it."

Sugartit stood up and undid her skirt zipper and began going into a slow striptease routine.

Sissie clutched her by the arms. "You stop that," she said. "You'd better go on home before your old man gets there first and comes out looking for you."

In a sudden rage, Sheik snatched Sissie's hands away from Sugartit and flung her across the bed.

"Leave her alone," he raved. "She's going to entertain the Sheik."

"If her old man's really Coffin Ed you oughta let her go on home," Sonny said soberly. "You just beggin' for trouble messin' round with his kinfolks."

"Choo-Choo, go to the kitchen and get Granny's wire clothesline," Sheik ordered.

Choo-Choo went out grinning.

When he saw Granny staring at him with such fierce disapproval, he said guiltily, "Pay no 'tention to me, Granny," and began clowning.

She didn't answer.

He tiptoed with elaborate pantomime to the closet and took out her coil of clothesline.

"Just wanna hang out the wash," he said.

Still she didn't answer.

He tiptoed close to the chair and passed his hand slowly in front of her face. She didn't bat an eyelash. His grin widened. Returning to the front room, he said, "Granny's dead asleep with her eyes wide open."

"Leave her to Gabriel," Sheik said, taking the line and beginning to uncoil it.

"What you gonna do with that?" Sonny asked apprehensively.

Sheik made a running loop in one end. "We going to play cowboy," he said. "Look."

Suddenly he threw the loop over Sonny's head and pulled on the line with all his strength. The loop tightened about Sonny's neck and jerked him off his feet.

Sissie ran toward Sheik and tried to pull the wire from his hands. "You're choking him," she said.

Sheik knocked her down with a backhanded blow.

"You can let up on him now," Choo-Choo said. "We got 'im."

"Now I'm gonna show you how to tie up a mother-raper to put him in a sack," Sheik said.

11

Grave Digger halted on the sidewalk in front of the yellow frame house next door to the Knickerbocker. It had been partitioned into offices and all of the front windows were lettered with business announcements.

"Can you read that writing on those windows?" Grave Digger asked Ready Belcher.

Ready glanced at him suspiciously. "Course I can read that writing."

"Read it then," Grave Digger said.

Ready stole another look. "Read what one?"

"Take your choice."

Ready squinted his good eye against the dark and read aloud, "*Joseph C. Clapp, Real Estate and Notary Public.*" He looked at Grave Digger like a dog who has retrieved a stick. "That one?"

"Try another."

He hesitated. Passing car lights played on his pock-marked black face, brought out the white cast in his bad eye and lit up his flashy tan suit.

"I haven't got much time," Grave Digger warned.

He read, "*Amazing 100-year-old Gypsy Bait Oil–Makes Catfish Go Crazy.*" He looked at Grave Digger again like the same dog with another stick.

"Not that one," Grave Digger said.

"What the hell is this, a gag?" he muttered.

"Just read!"

"*JOSEPH, The Only and Original Skin Lightener. I guarantee to lighten the darkest skin by twelve shades in six months.*"

"You don't want your skin lightened?"

"My skin suit me," he said sullenly.

"Then read on."

"*Magic Formula For Successful PRAYER* . . . That it?"

"Yeah, that's it. Read what it says underneath."

"*Here are some of the amazing things it tells you about: When to pray; Where to pray; How to pray; The Magic Formulas for Health and Success through prayer; for conquering fear through prayer; for obtaining work through prayer; for money through prayer; for influencing others through prayer; and –*"

"That's enough." Grave Digger took a deep breath and said in a voice gone thick and cottony again, "Ready, if you don't tell me what I want to know, you'd better get yourself one of those prayers. Because I'm going to take you over to 129th Street near the Harlem River. You know where that is? It's a deserted jungle of warehouses and junk yards beneath the New York Central bridge."

"Yare, I know where it's at."

"And I'm going to pistol whip you until your own whore won't recognize you again. And if you try to run, I'm going to let you run fifty feet and then shoot you through the head for attempting to escape. You understand me?"

"Yare, I understand you."

"You believe me?"

Ready took a quick look at Grave Digger's rage-swollen face and said quickly, "Yare, I believes you."

"My partner got suspended tonight for killing a criminal rat like you and I'd just as soon they suspended me too."

"You ain't asted me yet what you want to know."

"Get into the car."

The car was parked at the curb. Ready got into Coffin Ed's seat. Grave Digger went around and climbed beneath the wheel.

"This is as good a spot as any," he said. "Start talking."

" 'Bout what?"

"About the Big Greek. I want to know who killed him."

Ready jumped as though he'd been stung. "Digger, I swear 'fore God –"

"Don't call me Digger, you lousy pimp."

"Mista Jones, lissen –"

"I'm listening."

"Lots of folks mighta killed him if they'd knowed –" He broke off. The pockmarks in his skin began filling with sweat.

"Known what? I haven't got all night."

Ready gulped and said, "He was a whipper."

"What?"

"He liked to whip 'em."

"Whores?"

"Not 'specially. If they was regular whores he wanted them to be big black mannish-looking bitches like what might cut a mother-raper's throat. But what he liked most was little colored school gals."

"That's it? That's why Reba barred him?"

"Yas suh. He proposition her once. She got so mad she drew her pistol on him."

"Did she shoot him?"

"Naw, suh, she just scared him."

"I mean tonight. Was she the one?"

Ready's eyes started rolling in their sockets and the sweat began to trickle down his mean black face.

"You mean the one what killed him? Naw suh, she was home all evening."

"Where were you?"

"I was there, too."

"Do you live there?"

"Naw, suh, I just drops by for a visit now and then."

"Where did he find the girls?"

"You mean the school girls?"

"What other girls would I mean?"

"He picked 'em up in his car. He had a little Mexican bull whip with nine tails he kept in his car. He whipped 'em with that."

"Where did he take them?"

"He brung 'em to Reba's till she got suspicious 'bout all the screaming and carrying on. She didn't think nothing of it at first; these little chippies likes to make lots of noise for a white man. But they was making more noise than seemed natural and she went in and caught 'im. That's when he proposition her."

"How did he get 'em to take it?"

"Get 'em to take what?"

"The whipping."

"Oh, he paid 'em a hundred bucks. They was glad to take it for that."

"You're certain of that, that he paid them a hundred dollars?"

"Yas suh. Not only me but lots of chippies all over Harlem knew about him. A hundred bucks didn't mean nothing to him. They boy friends knew too. Lots of times they boy friends made 'em. There was chippies all over town on the lookout for him. 'Course one time was enough for most of 'em."

"He hurt them?"

"He got his money's worth. Sometime he whale hell out of 'em. I s'pect he hurt more'n one of 'em bad. 'Member that kid they picked up in Broadhurst Park. It were all in the paper. She was in the hospital three, four days. She said she'd been attacked but the police thought she was beat up by a gang. I believes she was one of 'em."

"What was her name?"

"I don't recollect."

"Where'd he take them after Reba barred him from her place?"

"I don't know."

"Do you know the names of any of them?"

"Naw suh, he brung 'em and took 'em away by hisself. I never even seen any of 'em."

"You're lying."

"Naw suh, I swear 'fore God."

"How did you know they were school girls if you never saw any of them?"

"He tole me."

"What else he tell you?"

"Nuthin' else. He just talk to me 'bout gals."

"How old is your girl?"

"My gal?"

"The one you have at Reba's?"

"Oh, she twenty-five or more."

"One more lie and off we go."

"She sixteen, boss."

"She had him, too?"

"Yas suh. Once."

The sweat was streaming down Ready's face.

"Once. Why only once?"

"She got scared."

"You tried to fix it up for another time?"

"Naw suh, boss, she didn't need to. Hit cost her more'n it was worth."

"What were you doing with him in the Dew Drop Inn?"

"He was looking for a little gal he knew and he ast me to come 'long, that's all, boss."

"When was that?"

" 'Bout a month ago."

"You said you didn't know where he took them after he was barred from Reba's."

"I don't, boss, I swear 'fore –"

"Can that Uncle Tom crap. Reba said she barred him three or four months ago."

"Yas suh, but I didn't say I hadn't seed him since."

"Did Reba know you were seeing him?"

"I only seed him that once, boss. I was in the Alabama-Georgia bar and he just happen in."

Grave Digger nodded towards the three alien cars parked ahead, in front of the Knickerbocker.

"One of those cars his?"

"Them struggle buggies!" Scorn pushed the fear from Ready's voice. "Naw suh, he had a dream boat, a big green Caddy Coupe de Ville."

"Who was the girl he and you were looking for?"

"I wasn't looking for her; I just went 'long with him to look for her."

"Who was she, I asked."

"I didn't know her. Some little chippie what hung 'round in that section."

"How did he come to know her?"

"He said he'd done whipped her girl friend once. That's how come he knew her. Said Sissie's boy friend brought her to 'im."

"Sissie! You said you didn't know the name of any of them."

"I'd forgotten her, boss. He didn't bring her to Reba's. I didn't know nuthin' 'bout her but just what he said."

"What did he say exactly?"

"He just say Sissie's boy friend, some boy they call Sheik, arrange it for him and he pay Sheik. Then he wanted Sheik to arrange for the other one but Sheik couldn't do it."

"What was the other one called? The one he and you were looking for?"

"He call her Sugartit. She was Sissie's girl friend. He'd seen 'em walking together down Seventh Avenue one time after he'd whipped Sissie."

"Where did you find her?"

"We didn't find her, I swear 'fore –"

"Does your girl know them?"

"I didn' hear you."

"Your girl, does she know them?"

"Know who, boss?"

"Either Sissie or Sugartit."

"Naw suh. My gal's a pro and them is just chippies. I recollect him saying one time they all belonged to a kid gang over in that section. I means them two chippies and Sheik. He say Sheik was the chief."

"What's the name of the gang?"
"He say they call themselves the Real Cool Moslems. He thought it were funny."
"Did you listen to the news on the radio tonight?"
"You mean what it say 'bout him getting croaked? Naw suh, I was lissening to the Twelve-Eighty Club. Reba tole me 'bout it. She were lissening. That were just 'fore you come. She were telling me when the doorbell rang. She say the big Greek's croaked over on Lenox Avenue and I say so what."
"You said before that lots of people might have killed him if they'd known about him. Who?"
"All I meant was some of those gal's pas. Like Sissie's or some of 'em. He might have been hanging 'round over there looking for Sugartit again and her pa might have got hep to it some kind of way and been layin' for him and when he seed him coming down the street might have lowered the boom on 'im."
"You mean slipped up behind him?"
"He were in his car, warn't he?"
"How about the Moslems – the kid gang?"
"Them! What they'd wanta do it for? He was money in the street for them."
"Who's Sugartit's father?"
"You mean her old man?"
"I mean her father."
"How am I gonna know that, boss? I ain't never heard of her 'fore he talk 'bout her."
"What did he say about her?"
"Just say she was the gal for him."
"Did he say where she lived?"
"Naw, suh, he just say what I say he say, boss, I swear 'fore God."
"You stink. What are you sweating so much for?"
"I'se just nervous, that's all."
"You stink with fear. What are you scared of?"
"Just naturally scared, boss. You got that big pistol and you mad at everybody and talkin' 'bout killin' me and all

that. Enough to make anybody scared."

"You're scared of something else, something in particular. What are you holding out?"

"I ain't holding nothing out. I done tole you everything I know, I swear boss, I swears on everything that's holy in this whole green world."

"I know you're lying. I can hear it in your voice. What are you lying about?"

"I ain't lying, boss. If I'm lying I hope God'll strike me dead on the spot."

"You know who her father is, don't you?"

"Naw suh, boss. I swear. I done tole you everything I know. You could whup me till my head is soft as clabber but I couldn't tell you no more than I'se already tole you."

"You know who her father is and you're scared to tell me."

"Naw suh, I swear –"

"Is he a politician?"

"Boss, I –"

"A numbers banker?"

"I swear, boss –"

"Shut up before I knock out your goddamned teeth."

He mashed the starter as though tromping on Ready's head. The motor purred into life. But he didn't slip in the clutch. He sat there listening to the softly purring motor in the small black nondescript car, trying to get his temper under control.

Finally he said, "If I find out that you're lying I'm going to kill you like a dog. I'm not going to shoot you, I'm going to break all your bones. I'm going to try to find out who killed Galen because that's what I'm paid for and that was my oath when I took this job. But if I had my way I'd pin a medal on him and I'd string up every goddamned one of you who were up with Galen. You've turned my stomach and it's all I can do right now to keep from beating out your brains."

12

The reception room of the Harlem Hospital, on Lenox Avenue ten blocks south from the scene of the murder, was wrapped in a midnight hush.

It was called an interracial hospital; more than half of its staff of doctors and nurses were colored people.

A graduate nurse sat behind the reception desk. A bronze-shaded desk lamp spilled light on the hospital register before her while her brown-skinned face remained in shadow. She looked up inquiringly as Grave Digger and Ready Belcher approached, walking side by side.

"May I help you," she said in a trained courteous voice.

"I'm Detective Jones," Grave Digger said, exhibiting his badge.

She looked at it but didn't touch it.

"You received an emergency patient here about two hours ago; a man with his right arm cut off."

"Yes?"

"I would like to question him."

"I will call Dr. Banks. You may talk to him. Please be seated."

Grave Digger prodded Ready in the direction of chairs surrounding a table with magazines. They sat silently, like relatives of a critical case.

Dr. Banks came in silently, crossing the linoleum-tiled floor on rubber-soled shoes. He was a tall, athletic-looking young colored man dressed in white.

"I'm sorry to have kept you waiting, Mr. Jones," he said to Grave Digger whom he knew by sight. "You want to know about the case with the severed arm." He had a quick smile and a pleasant voice.

"I want to talk to him," Grave Digger said.

Dr. Banks pulled up a chair and sat down. "He's dead. I've just come from him. He had a rare type of blood – Type O – which we don't have in our blood bank. You realize transfusions were imperative. We had to contact the Red Cross blood bank. They located the type in Brooklyn, but it arrived too late. Is there anything I can tell you?"

"I want to know who he was."

"So do we. He died without revealing his identity."

"Didn't he make a statement of any kind before he died?"

"There was another detective here earlier, but the patient was unconscious at the time. The patient regained consciousness later, but the detective had left. Before leaving, he examined the patient's effects, however, but found nothing to establish his identity."

"He didn't talk at all, didn't say anything?"

"Oh yes. He cried a great deal. One moment he was cursing and the next he was praying. Most of what he said was incoherent. I gathered he regretted not killing the man whom he had attacked – the white man who was killed later."

"He didn't mention any names?"

"No. Once he said 'the little one' but mostly he used the word *mother-raper* which Harlemites apply to everybody, enemies, friends and strangers."

"Well, that's that," Grave Digger said. "Whatever he knew he took with him. Still I'd like to examine his effects too, whatever they are."

"Certainly; they're just the clothes he wore and the contents of his pockets when he arrived here." He stood up. "Come this way."

Grave Digger got to his feet and motioned his head for Ready to walk ahead of him.

"Are you an officer too?" Dr. Banks asked Ready.

"No, he's my prisoner," Grave Digger said. "We're not that hard up for cops as yet."

Dr. Banks smiled. He led them down a corridor smelling strongly of ether to a room at the far end where the clothes and personal effects of the emergency and ward patients were stored in neatly wrapped bundles on shelves against the walls. He took down a bundle bearing a metal tag and placed it on the bare wooden table.

"Here you are."

From the adjoining room an anguished male voice was heard reciting the Lord's Prayer.

Ready stared as though fascinated at the number 219 on the metal tag fastened to the bundle of clothes and whispered, "Death row."

Dr. Banks flicked a glance at him and said to Grave Digger, "Most of the attendants play the numbers. When an emergency patient arrives they put this tag with the death number on his bundle and if he dies they play it."

Grave Digger grunted and began untying the bundle.

"If you discover anything leading to his identity, let us know," Dr. Banks said. "We'd like to notify his relatives." He left them.

Grave Digger spread the blood-caked mackinaw and overalls on the table. It contained two incredibly filthy one-dollar bills, some loose change, a small brown paper sack of dried roots, two Yale keys and a skeleton key on a rusty key ring, a dried rabbit's foot, a dirty piece of resin, a cheese cloth rag that had served as a handkerchief, a putty knife, a small piece of pumice stone, and a scrap of dirty writing paper folded into a small square. The putty knife and pumice stone indicated that the man had worked somewhere as a porter, using the putty to scrape chewing gum from the floor and the pumice stone for cleaning his hands. That didn't help much.

He unfolded the square of paper and found a note on cheap school paper written in a childish hand.

> GB, you want to know something. The Big John hangs out in the Inn. How about that. Just like those old Romans.
> Bee.

Grave Digger folded it again and slipped it into his pocket.

"Is your girl called Bee?" he asked Ready.

"Naw, suh, she called Doe."

"Do you know any girl called Bee – a school girl?"

"Naw suh."

"GB?"

"Naw suh."

Grave Digger turned out the pockets of the clothes but found nothing more. He wrapped the bundle and attached the tag. He noticed Ready staring at the number on the tag again.

"Don't let that number catch up with you," he said. "Don't you end up with that tag on your fine clothes."

Ready licked his dry lips.

They didn't see Dr. Banks on their way out. Grave Digger stopped at the reception desk to tell the nurse he hadn't found anything to identify the corpse.

"Now we're going to look for the Greek's car," he said to Ready.

They found the big green Cadillac beneath a street lamp in the middle of the block on 130th Street between Lenox and Seventh Avenues. It had an Empire State license number – UG-16 – and it was parked beside a fire hydrant. It was as conspicuous as a fire truck.

He pulled up behind it and parked.

"Who covered for him in Harlem?" he asked Ready.

"I don't know, Mista Jones."

"Was it the precinct captain?"

"Mista Jones, I –"

"One of our councilmen?"

"Honest to God, Mista Jones –"

Grave Digger got out and walked toward the big car.

The doors were locked. He broke the glass of the left-side wind screen with the butt of his pistol, reached inside past the wheel and unlocked the door. The interior lights came on.

A quick search revealed the usual paraphernalia of a motorist: gloves, handkerchiefs, Kleenex, half-used packages of different brands of cigarettes, insurance papers, a woman's plastic overshoes and compact. A felt monkey dangled from the rear view mirror and two medium-sized dolls, a black-faced Topsy and a blonde Little Eva, sat in opposite corners on the back seat.

He found the miniature bull whip and a Manila envelope of postcard-sized photos in the right-hand glove compartment. He studied the photos in the light. They were pictures of nude colored girls in various postures, each photo revealing another developed technique of the sadist. On most of the pictures the faces of the girls were distinct although distorted by pain and shame.

He put the whip in his leather-lined coat pocket, kept the photos in his hand, slammed the door, walked back to his own car and climbed beneath the wheel.

"Was he a photographer?" he asked Ready.

"Yas suh, sometime he carry a camera."

"Did he show you the pictures he took?"

"Naw suh, he never said nothing 'bout any pictures. I just seen him with the camera."

Grave Digger snapped on the top light and showed Ready the photos.

"Do you recognize any of them?"

Ready whistled softly and his eyes popped as he turned over one photo after another.

"Naw suh, I don't know none of them," he said, handing them back.

"Your girl's not one of them?"

"Naw suh."

Grave Digger pocketed the envelope and mashed the starter.

"Ready, don't let me catch you in a lie," he said again, letting out the clutch.

13

He parked directly in front of the Dew Drop Inn and pushed Ready through the door. On first sight it looked just as he had left it; the two white cops guarding the door and the colored patrons celebrating noisily. He ushered Ready between the bar and the booths, toward the rear. The vari-colored faces turned toward them curiously as they passed.

But in the last booth he noticed an addition. It was crowded with teenagers, three school boys and four school girls, who hadn't been there before. They stopped talking and looked at him intently as he and Ready approached. Then at sight of the bull whip all four girls gave a start and their young dark faces tightened with sudden fear. He wondered how they'd got past the white cops on the door.

All the places at the bar were taken.

Big Smiley came down and asked two men to move.

One of them began to complain. "What for I got to give up my seat for some other niggers."

Big Smiley thumbed toward Grave Digger. "He's the man."

"Oh, one of them two."

Both rose with alacrity, picked up their glasses and vacated the stools, grinning at Grave Digger obsequiously.

"Don't show me your teeth," Grave Digger snarled. "I'm no dentist. I don't fix teeth. I'm a cop. I'll knock your teeth out."

The men doused their grins and slunk away.

Grave Digger threw the bull whip on top of the bar and sat on the high bar stool.

"Sit down," he ordered Ready, who stood by hesitantly. "Sit down, Goddamn it."

Ready sat down as though the stool were covered with

cake icing.

Big Smiley looked from one to another, smiling warily.

"You held out on me," Grave Digger said in his thick cottony voice of smoldering rage. "And I don't like that."

Big Smiley's smile got a sudden case of constipation. He threw a quick look at Ready's impassive face, found nothing there to reassure him, then fell back on his cut arm which he carried in a sling.

"Guess I must be runnin' some fever, Chief, 'cause I don't remember what I told you."

"You told me you didn't know who Galen was looking for in here," Grave Digger said thickly.

Big Smiley stole another look at Ready, but all he got was a blank. He sighed heavily.

"Who he were looking for? Is dat what you ast me?" he stalled, trying to meet Grave Digger's smoldering hot gaze. "I dunno who he were looking for, Chief."

Grave Digger rose up on the bar stool rungs as though his feet were in stirrups, snatched the bull whip from the bar and slashed Big Smiley across one cheek after another before Big Smiley could get his good hand moving.

Big Smiley stopped smiling. Talk stopped suddenly along the length of the bar, petered out in the booths. In the vacuum that followed, Lil Green's voice whined from the jukebox:

"Why don't you do right
Like other mens do . . ."

Grave Digger sat back on the stool, breathing hard, struggling to control his rage. Veins stood out in his temples, growing out of his short-cropped kinky hair like strange roots climbing toward the brim of his misshapen hat. His brown eyes laced with red veins generated a steady white heat.

The white manager, who'd been working the front end of the bar, hastened down toward them with a face full of outrage.

"Get back," Grave Digger said thickly.

The manager got back.

Grave Digger stabbed at Big Smiley with his left forefinger and said in a voice so thick it was hard to understand, "Smiley, all I want from you is the truth. And I ain't got long to get it."

Big Smiley didn't look at Ready any more. He didn't smile. He didn't whine.

He said, "Just ask the questions, Chief, and I'll answer 'em the best of my knowledge."

Grave Digger looked around at the teenagers in the booth. They were listening with open mouths, staring at him with popping eyes. His breath burned from his flaring nostrils. He turned back to Big Smiley. But he sat quietly for a moment to give the blood time to recede from his head.

"Who killed him?" he finally asked.

"I don't know, Chief."

"He was killed on your street."

"Yas suh, but I don't know who done it."

"Do Sissie and Sugartit come in here?"

"Yas suh, sometimes."

Out of the corners of his eyes Grave Digger noticed Ready's shoulders begin to sag as though his spine were melting.

"Sit up straight, God damn it," he said. "You'll have plenty of time to lie down if I find out you've been lying."

Ready sat up straight.

Grave Digger addressed Big Smiley. "Galen met them in here?"

"Naw suh, he met Sissie in here once but I never seen him with Sugartit."

"What was she doing in here then?"

"She come in here twice with Sissie."

"How'd you know her name?"

"I heard Sissie call her that."

"Was Sheik with her when Galen met her?"

"You mean with Sissie, when she met the big man? Yas

suh."

"He paid Sheik the money?"

"I couldn't be sure, Chief, but I seen money being passed. I don't know who got it."

"He got it. Did they both leave with him?"

"You mean both Sheik and Sissie?"

"That's what I mean."

Big Smiley took out a blue bandana handkerchief and mopped his sweating black face.

The four school girls in the booth began going through the motions of leaving. Grave Digger wheeled toward them.

"Sit down! I want to talk to you later," he ordered.

They began a shrill protest: "We got to get home . . . Got to be at school tomorrow at nine o'clock . . . Haven't finished homework . . . Can't stay out this late . . . Get into trouble . . ."

He got up and went over to show them his gold badge. "You're already in trouble. Now I want you to sit down and keep quiet."

He took hold of the two girls who were standing and forced them back into their seats.

"He can't hold you 'less he's got a warrant," the boy in the aisle seat said.

Grave Digger slapped him out of his seat, reached down and lifted him from the floor by his coat lapels and slammed him back into his seat.

"Now say that again," he suggested.

The boy didn't speak.

Grave Digger waited for a moment until they had settled down and were quiet, then he returned to his bar stool.

Neither Big Smiley nor Ready had moved; neither had looked at the other.

"You didn't answer my question," Grave Digger said.

"When he took Sissie off Sheik stayed in his seat," Big Smiley said.

"What kind of a goddamned answer is that?"

"That's the way it was, Chief."

"Where did he take her?"
Rivers of sweat poured from Big Smiley's face. He sighed. "Downstairs," he said.
"Downstairs! In here?"
"Yas suh. They's stairs in the back room."
"What's downstairs?"
"Just a cellar like any other bar's got. It's full of bottles an' old bar fixtures and beer barrels. The compression unit for the draught beer is down there and the refrigeration unit for the ice boxes. That's all. Some rats and we keeps a cat."
"No bed or bedroom?"
"Naw suh."
"He whipped them down there in that kind of place?"
"I don't know what he done."
"Couldn't you hear them?"
"Naw suh. You can't hear nothin' through this floor. You could shoot off your pistol down there and you couldn't hear it up here."
Grave Digger looked at Ready. "Did you know that?"
Ready began to wilt again. "Naw suh, I swear 'fore –"
"Sit up straight, God damn it! I don't want to have to tell you again."
He turned back to Big Smiley. "Did he know it?"
"Not so far as I know, unless he told him."
"Is Sissie or Sugartit among those girls over there?"
"Naw suh," Big Smiley said without looking.
Grave Digger showed him the pornographic photos. "Know any of them?"
Big Smiley leafed through them slowly without a change of expression. He pulled out three photos. "I've seen them," he said.
"What're their names?"
"I don't know only two of 'em." He separated them gingerly with his fingertips as though they were coated with external poison. "Them two. This here one is called Good Booty, t'other one is called Honey Bee. This one here, I never heard her name called."

"What are their family names?"
"I don't know none of 'em's square monicker's."
"He took these downstairs?"
"Just them two."
"Who came here with them?"
"They came by theyself, most of 'em did."
"Did he have appointments with them?"
"Naw suh, not with most of 'em, anyway. They just come in here and laid for him."
"Did they come together?"
"Sometime, sometime not."
"You just said they came by themselves."
"I meant they didn't bring no boy friends."
"Had he known them before?"
"I couldn't say. When he come in if he seed any of 'em he just made his choice."
"He knew they hung around here looking for him?"
"Yas suh. When he started comin' here he was already known."
"When was that?"
"Three or four months ago. I don't remember 'zactly."
"When did he start taking them downstairs?"
" 'Bout two months ago."
"Did you suggest it?"
"Naw suh, he propositioned me."
"How much did he pay you?"
"Twenty-five bucks."
"You're talking yourself into Sing-Sing."
"Maybe."
Grave Digger examined the note addressed to GB and signed Bee that he'd taken from the dead man's effects, then passed it over to Big Smiley.
"That came from the pocket of the man you cut," he said.
Big Smiley read the note carefully, his lips spelling out each word. His breath came out in a sighing sound.
"Then he must be a relation of her," he said.
"You didn't know that?"

"Naw suh, I swear 'fore God. If I knowed that I wouldn't 'ave chopped him with the axe."

"What exactly did he say to Galen when he started toward him with the knife?"

Big Smiley wrinkled his forehead. "I don't 'member 'zactly. Something 'bout if he found a white mother-raper trying to diddle his little gals he'd cut his throat. But I just took that to mean colored women in general. You know how our folks talk. I didn't figure he meant his own kin."

"Maybe some other girl's father had the same idea with a pistol," Grave Digger suggested.

"Could be," Big Smiley said cautiously.

"So evidently he's the father and he's got more girls than one."

"Looks like it."

"He's dead."

Big Smiley's expression didn't change. "I'm sorry to hear it."

"You look like it. Who went your bail?"

"My boss."

Grave Digger looked at him soberly. "Who's covering for you?" he asked.

"Nobody."

"I know that's a lie but I'm going to pass it. Who was covering for Galen?"

"I don't know."

"I'm going to pass that lie too. What was he doing here tonight?"

"He was looking for Sugartit."

"Did he have a date with her?"

"I don't know. He said she was coming by with Sissie."

"Did they come by after he'd left?"

"Naw suh."

"Okay, Smiley, this one is for keeps. Who is Sugartit's father?"

"I don't know none of 'em's kinfolks nor neither where they lives, Chief, like I told you before. It didn't make no difference."

"You must have some idea."

"Naw suh, it's just like I say, I never thought about it. You don't never think 'bout where a gal lives in Harlem, 'less you goin' home with her. What do anybody's address mean up here?"

"Don't let me catch you in a lie, Smiley."

"I ain't lying, Chief. I went with a woman for a whole year once and never did know where she lived. Didn't care neither."

"Who are the Real Cool Moslems?"

"Them punks! Just a kid gang around here."

"Where do they hang out?"

"I don't know 'zactly. Somewhere down the street."

"Do they come in here?"

"Only three of 'em sometime. Sheik – I think he's they leader – and a boy called Choo-Choo and the one they call Bones."

"Where do they live?"

"Somewhere near here, but I don't know 'zactly. The boy what keeps the pigeons oughtta know. He lives a coupla blocks down the street on t'other side. I don't know his name but he got a pigeon coop on the roof."

"Is he one of 'em?"

"I don't know for sure but you can see a gang of boys on the roof when he's flying his pigeons."

"I'll find him. Do you know the ages of those girls in the booth?"

"Naw suh, when I ask 'em they say they're eighteen."

"You know they're under age."

"I s'pect so but all I can do is ast 'em."

"Did he have any of them?"

"Only one I knows of."

Grave Digger turned and looked at the girls again.

"Which one?" he asked.

"The one in the green tam." Big Smiley pushed forward one of the three photos. "She's this one here, the one called

Good Booty."

"Okay, son, that's all for the moment," Grave Digger said.

He got down from the stool and walked forward to talk to the manager.

As soon as he left, without saying a word or giving a warning Big Smiley leaned forward and hit Ready in the face with his big ham-sized fist. Ready sailed off the stool, crashed into the wall and crumpled to the floor.

Grave Digger looked down in time to see his head disappearing beneath the edge of the bar, then turned his attention to the white manager across from him.

"Collect your tabs and shut the bar; I'm closing up this joint and you're under arrest," he said.

"For what?" the manager challenged hotly.

"For contributing to the delinquency of minors."

The manager sputtered, "I'll be open again by tomorrow night."

"Don't say another God damned word," Grave Digger said and kept looking at him until the manager closed his mouth and turned away.

Then he beckoned to one of the white cops on the door and told him, "I'm putting the manager and the bartender under arrest and closing the joint. I want you to hold the manager and some teenagers I'll turn over to you. I'm going to leave in a minute and I'll send back the wagon. I'll take the bartender with me."

"Right, Jones," the cop said, as happy as a kid with a new toy.

Grave Digger walked back to the rear.

Ready was down on the floor on his hands and knees, spitting out blood and teeth.

Grave Digger looked at him and smiled grimly. Then he looked up at Big Smiley who was licking his bruised knuckles with a big red tongue.

"You're under arrest, Smiley," he said. "If you try to escape, I'm going to shoot you through the back of the

head."
"Yas suh," Big Smiley said.
Grave Digger shook a customer loose from a plastic-covered chair and sat astride it at the end of the table in the booth, facing the scared, silent teenagers. He took out his notebook and stylo and wrote down their names, addresses, numbers of the public schools they attended, and their ages. The oldest was a boy of seventeen.
None of them admitted knowing either Sissie, Sugartit, the big white man Galen, or anyone connected with the Real Cool Moslems.
He called the second cop away from the door and said, "Hold these kids for the wagon."
Then he said to the girl in the green tam who'd given her name as Gertrude B. Richardson. "Gertrude, I want you to come with me."
One of the girls tittered. "You might have known he'd take Good Booty," she said.
"My name is Beauty," Good Booty said, tossing her head disdainfully.
On sudden impulse Grave Digger stopped her as she was about to get up.
"What's your father's name, Gertrude?"
"Charlie."
"What does he do?"
"He's a porter."
"Is that so? Do you have any sisters?"
"One. She's a year younger than me."
"What does your mother do?"
"I don't know. She don't live with us."
"I see. You two girls live with your father."
"Where else we going to live?"
"That's a good question, Gertrude, but I can't answer it. Did you know a man got his arm cut off in here earlier tonight?"
"I heard about it. So what? People are always getting cut around here."

"This man tried to knife the white man because of his daughters."

"He did?" She giggled. "He was a square."

"No doubt. The bartender chopped off his arm with an axe to protect the white man. What do you think about that?"

She giggled again, nervously. "Maybe he figured the white man was more important than some colored drunk."

"He must have. The man died in Harlem Hospital less than an hour ago."

Her eyes got big and frightened. "What are you trying to say, mister?"

"I'm trying to tell you that he was your father."

Grave Digger hadn't anticipated her reaction. She came up out of her seat so fast that she was past him before he could grab her.

"Stop her!" he shouted.

A customer wheeled from his bar stool into her path and she stuck her fingers into his eye. The man yelped and tried to hold her. She wrenched from his grip and sprang towards the door. The white cop headed her off and wrapped his arms about her. She twisted in his grip like a panic-stricken cat and clawed at his pistol. She had gotten it out the holster when a colored man rushed in and wrenched it from her grip. The white cop threw her onto the floor on her back and straddled her, pinning down her arms. The colored man grabbed her by the feet. She writhed on her back and spat into the cop's face.

Grave Digger came up and looked down at her from sad brown eyes. "It's too late now, Gertrude," he said. "They're both dead."

Suddenly she began to cry. "What did he have to mess in it for?" she sobbed. "Oh, Pa, what did you have to mess in it for?"

14

Two uniformed white cops standing guard on a dark rooftop were talking.

"Do you think we'll find him?"

"Do I think we'll find him? Do you know who we're looking for? Have you stopped to think for a moment that we're looking for one colored man who supposedly is handcuffed and seven other colored men who were wearing green turbans and false beards when last seen. Have you turned that over in your mind? By this time they've got rid of those phony disguises and maybe Pickens has got rid of his handcuffs too. And then what does that make them, I ask you? That makes them just like eighteen thousand or one hundred and eighty thousand other colored men, all looking alike. Have you ever stopped to think there are five hundred thousand colored people in Harlem – one half of a million people with black skin. All looking alike. And we're trying to pick eight out of them. It's like trying to find a cinder in a coal bin. It ain't possible."

"Do you think all these colored people in this neighbourhood know who Pickens and the Moslems are?"

"Sure they know. Every last one of them. Unless some other colored person turns Pickens in he'll never be found. They're laughing at us."

"As much as the chief wants that coon, whoever finds him is sure to get a promotion," the first cop said.

"Yeah, I know, but it ain't possible," the second cop said. "If that coon's got any sense at all he would have filed those cuffs in two a long time ago."

"What good would that do him if he couldn't get them off?"

"Hell, he could wear heavy gloves with gauntlets like –

Hey! Didn't we see some coon wearing driving gauntlets?"

"Yeah, that halfwit coon with the pigeons."

"Wearing gauntlets and a ragged old overcoat. And a coal black coon at that. He certainly fits the description."

"That halfwitted coon. You think it's possible he's the one?"

"Come on! What are we waiting for?"

Sheik said, "Now all we've got to do is get this mother-raper past the police lines and throw him into the river."

"Doan do that to me, please, Sheik," Sonny's muffled voice pleaded from inside the sack.

"Shhhh," Choo-Choo cautioned. "Chalk the walking Jeffs."

The two cops leaned over and peered in through the open window.

"Where's that boy who was wearing gloves?" the first cop asked.

"Gloves!" Choo-Choo echoed, going into his clowning act like a chameleon changing color. "You means boxing gloves?"

The second cop sniffed. "A weed pad!" he exclaimed.

They climbed inside. Their gazes swept quickly over the room.

The roof reeked of marijuana smoke. Everyone was high. The ones who hadn't smoked were high from inhaling the smoke and watching the eccentric motions of the ones who had smoked.

"Who's got the sticks?" the first cop demanded.

"Come on, come on, who's got the sticks?" the second cop echoed, looking from one to the other. He passed over Sheik who stood in the center of the floor where he'd been arrested in motion by Choo-Choo's warning and stared at them as though trying to make out what they were; then over Inky who was caught in the act of ducking behind the curtains in the corner and stood there half in and half out, like a billboard advertisement for a movie about bad girls;

and landed on Choo-Choo who seemed the most vulnerable because he was grinning like an idiot. "You got the sticks, boy?"

"Sticks! You mean that there pigeon stick," Choo-Choo said, pointing at the bamboo pole on the floor beside the bed.

"Don't get funny with me, boy!"

"I just don't know what you means, boss."

"Forget the sticks," the first cop said. "Let's find the boy with the gloves."

He looked about. His gaze lit on Sugartit who was sitting in the straight-backed chair and staring with a fixed expression at what appeared to be a gunny sack filled with huge lumps of coal lying in the middle of the bed.

"What's in that sack?" he asked suspiciously.

For an instant no one replied.

Then Choo-Choo said, "Just some coal."

"On the bed?"

"It's clean coal."

The cop pinned a threatening look on him.

"It's my bed," Sheik said. "I can put what I want on it."

Both cops turned to stare at him.

"You're a kind of lippy bastard," the first cop said. "What's your name?"

"Samson."

"You live here?"

"Right here."

"Then you're the boy we're looking for. That's your pigeon loft on the roof."

"No, that's not him," the second cop said. "The boy we want is blacker than he is and has another name."

"What's a name to these coons?" the first cop said. "They're always changing about."

"No, the one we want is called Inky. He was the one wearing the gloves."

"Now I remember. He was called Caleb. He was the one wearing the gloves. The other one was Inky, the one who couldn't talk."

The second cop wheeled on Sheik. "Where's Caleb?"

"I don't know anybody named Caleb."

"The hell you don't! He lives here with you."

"Naw suh, you means that boy what lives down on the first floor," Choo-Choo said.

"Don't tell me what I mean. I mean the boy who lives here on this floor. He's the boy who's got the pigeon loft."

"Naw suh, boss, if you means the Caleb what's got the pigeon roost, he lives on the first floor."

"Don't lie to me, boy. I saw the sergeant bring him down the fire escape to this floor."

"Naw suh, boss, the sergeant taken him on by this floor and carried him down on the fire escape to the first floor. We seen 'em when they come by the window. Didn't we, Amos?" he called to Inky.

"That's right, suh," Inky said. "They went right past that window there."

"What other window could they go by?"

"None other window, suh."

"They had another boy with 'em called Inky," Choo-Choo said. "It looked like they had 'em both arrested."

The second cop was staring at Inky. "This boy here looks like Inky to me," he said. "Aren't you Inky, boy?"

"Naw suh –" Inky began, but Choo-Choo quickly cut him off: "They calls him Smokey. Inky is the other one."

"Let him talk for himself," the first said.

The second cop pinned another threatening look on Choo-Choo. "Are you trying to make a fool out of me, boy!"

"Naw suh, boss, I'se just tryin' a help."

"Let up on him," the first cop said. "These coons are jagged on weed; they're not strictly responsible."

"Responsible or not, they'd better be careful before they get some lumps on their heads."

The first cop noticed Sissie standing quietly in the corner, holding her hand to her bruised cheek.

"You know them, Caleb and Inky, don't you girl?" he asked her.

"No sir, I just know Smokey," she said.

Suddenly Sonny sneezed.

Sugartit giggled.

The cop wheeled toward the bed, looked at the sack and then looked at her.

"Who was that sneezed?"

She put her hand to her mouth and tried to stop laughing.

The cop turned slightly pinkish and drew his pistol.

"Someone's underneath the bed," he said. "Keep the other covered while I look."

The second cop drew his pistol.

"Just relax and no one will get hurt," he said calmly.

The first cop got down on his hands and knees, holding his cocked pistol ready to shoot, and looked underneath the bed.

Sugartit put both hands over her mouth and bit into her palm. Her face swelled with suppressed laughter and tears flowed down her cheeks.

The cop straightened to his knees and braced himself on the edge of the bed. There was a perplexed look on his red face.

"There's something funny going on here," he said. "There's someone else in this room."

"Ain't nobody here but us ghosts, boss," Choo-Choo said.

The cop threw him a look of frustrated fury, and started to his feet.

"By God, I'll –" His voice dried up when he heard the choking sounds issuing from inside the sack.

He jumped upward and backward as though one of the ghosts had sure enough groaned. Leveling his pistol, he said in a quaking voice, "What's in that sack?"

Sugartit burst into hysterical laughter.

For an instant no one spoke.

Then Choo-Choo said hastily, "Hit's just Joe."

"What!"

"Hit's just Joe in the sack."

"Joe!"

Gingerly, the cop leaned over, holding his cocked pistol in his right hand, and with his left untied the cord closing the sack. He drew the top of the sack open.

Popping eyes in a gray-black face stared up at him.

The cop drew back in horror. His face turned white and a shudder passed over his big solid frame.

"It's a body," he said in a choked voice. "All trussed up."

"Hit ain't no body, hit's just Joe," Choo-Choo said, not intending to play the comic.

The second cop hastened over to look. "It's still alive," he said.

"He's choking!" Sissie cried and ran over and began loosening the noose about Sonny's neck.

Sonny sucked in breath with a gasp.

"My God, what's he doing in there?" the first cop asked in amazement.

"He's just studying magic," Choo-Choo said. He was beginning to sweat from the strain.

"Magic!"

The second cop noticed Sheik inching toward the window and aimed his pistol at him.

"Oh no, you don't," he said. "You come over here."

Sheik turned and came closer.

"Studying magic!" the first cop said. "In a sack?"

"Yas suh, he's trying to learn how to get out, like Houdini."

Color flooded back into the cop's face. "I ought to take him in for indecent exposure," he said.

"Hell, he's wearing a sack, ain't he," the second cop said, amused by his own wit.

Both of them grinned at Sonny as though he were a harmless halfwit.

Then the second cop said suddenly, "It ain't possible! There can't be two such halfwits in the whole world."

The first cop looked closely at Sonny and said slowly, "I believe you're right." Then to the others at large, "Get that boy out of that sack."

Sheik didn't move, but Choo-Choo and Inky hastened over and pulled Sonny out while Sissie held the bottom of the sack.

The cops stared at Sonny in awe.

"Looks like barbecued coon, don't he?" the first cop said.

Sugartit burst into laughter again.

Sonny's black skin had a gray pallor as though he'd been dusted over lightly with wood ash. He was shaking like a leaf.

The second cop reached out and turned him around.

Everyone stared at the handcuff bracelets clamped about each wrist.

"That's our boy," the first cop said.

"Lawd, suh, I wish I'd gone home and gone to bed," Sonny said in a moaning voice.

"I'll bet you do," the cop said.

Sugartit couldn't stop laughing.

15

The bodies had been taken to the morgue. All that remained were chalk outlines on the pavement where they had lain.

The street had been cleared of private cars. Police tow trucks had carried away those that had been abandoned in the middle of the street. Most of the patrol cars had returned to duty; those remaining blocked the area.

The chief of police's car occupied the center of the stage. It was parked in the middle of the intersection of 127th Street and Lenox Avenue.

To one side of it, the chief, Lieutenant Anderson, the lieutenant from homicide and the precinct sergeant who'd led one of the search parties were grouped about the boy called Bones.

The lieutenant from homicide had a zip gun in his hand.

"All right then, it isn't yours," he said to Bones in a voice of tried patience. "Whose is it then? Who were you hiding it for?"

Bones stole a glance at the lieutenant's face and his gaze dropped quickly to the street. It crawled over the four pairs of big black copper's boots. They looked like the Sixth Fleet at anchor. He didn't answer.

He was a slim black boy of medium height with girlish features and short hair almost straight at the roots and parted on one side. He wore a natty topcoat over his sweat shirt and tight-fitting black pants above shiny tan pointed-toed shoes.

An elderly man, a head taller, with a face grizzled from hard outdoor work, stood beside him. Kinky hair grew like burdock weeds on his shiny black dome, and worried brown eyes looked down at Bones from behind steel-rimmed spectacles.

"Go 'head, tell 'em, so, don't be no fool," he said; then he looked up and saw Grave Digger approaching with his prisoners. "Here comes Digger Jones," he said. "You can tell him, cain't you?"

Everybody looked about.

Grave Digger held Good Booty by the arm and Big Smiley and Ready Belcher, handcuffed together, were walking in front of him.

He looked at Anderson and said, "I closed up the Dew Drop Inn. The manager and some juvenile delinquents are being held by the officers on duty. You'd better send a wagon up there."

Anderson whistled for a patrol car team and gave them the order.

"What did you find out on Galen?" the chief asked.

"I found out he was a pervert," Grave Digger said.

"It figures," the homicide lieutenant said.

The chief turned red. "I don't give a goddamn what he was," he said. "Have you found out who killed him?"

"No, right now I'm still guessing at it," Grave Digger said.

"Well, guess fast then. I'm getting goddamned tired of standing up here watching this comedy of errors."

"I'll give you a quick fill-in and let you guess too," Grave Digger said.

"Well, make it short and sweet and I damn sure ain't going to guess," the chief said.

"Listen, Digger," the colored civilian interposed. "You and me is both city workers. Tell 'em my boy ain't done no harm."

"He's broken the Sullivan law concerning concealed weapons by having this gun in his possession," the homicide lieutenant said.

"That little thing," Bones's father said scornfully. "I don't b'lieve that'll even shoot."

"Get these people away from here and let Jones report," the chief said testily.

"Well, do something with them, Sergeant," Lieutenant Anderson said.

"Come on, both of you," the sergeant said, taking the man by the arm.

"Digger –" the man appealed.

"It'll keep," Grave Digger said harshly. "Your boy belonged to the Moslem gang."

"Naw-naw, Digger –"

"Do I have to slug you," the sergeant said.

The man allowed himself to be taken along with his son across the street.

The sergeant turned them over to a corporal and hurried back. Before he'd gone three steps the corporal was summoning two cops to take charge of them.

"What kind of city work does he do?" the chief asked.

"He's in the sanitation department," the sergeant said. "He's a garbage collector."

"All right, get on Jones," the chief ordered.

"Galen picked up colored school girls, teenagers, and took them to a crib on 145th Street," Grave Digger said in a flat toneless voice.

"Did you close it?" the Chief asked.

"It'll keep; I'm looking for a murderer now," Grave Digger said. Taking the miniature bull whip from his pocket, he went on, "He whipped them with this."

The chief reached out silently and took it from his hand.

"Have you got a list of the girls, Jones?" he asked.

"What for?"

"There might be a connection."

"I'm coming to that –"

"Well, get to it then."

"The landprop, a woman named Reba – used to call herself Sheba – the one who testified against Captain Murphy –"

"Ah, that one," the chief said softly. "She won't slip out of this."

"She'll take somebody with her," Grave Digger warned. "She's covered and Galen was, too."

The chief looked at Lieutenant Anderson reflectively.

The silence ran on until the sergeant blurted, "That's not in this precinct."

Anderson looked at the sergeant. "No one's charging you with it."

"Get on, Jones," the chief said.

"Reba got scared of the deal and barred him. Her story will be that she barred him when she found out what he was doing. But that's neither here nor there. After she barred him Galen started meeting them in the Dew Drop Inn. He arranged with the bartender so he could whip them in the cellar."

Everyone except Grave Digger seemed embarrassed.

"He ran into a girl named Sissie," Grave Digger said. "How doesn't matter at the moment. She's the girl friend of a boy called Sheik, who is the leader of the Real Cool Moslems."

Sudden tension took hold of the group.

"Sheik sold Sissie to him. Then Galen wanted Sissie's girl friend Sugartit. Sheik couldn't get Sugartit, but Galen kept looking for her in the neighbourhood. I have the bartender here and a two-bit pimp who has a girl at Reba's. He steered for Galen. I got this much from them."

The officers stared appraisingly at the two handcuffed prisoners.

"If they know that much, they know who killed him," the chief said.

"It's going to be their asses if they do," Grave Digger said. "But I think they're leveling. The way I figure it, the whole thing hinges on Sugartit. I think he was killed because of her."

"By who?"

"That's the jackpot question."

The chief looked at Good Booty. "Is this girl Sugartit?"

The others stared at her, too.

"No, she's another one."

"Who is Sugartit then?"

"I haven't found out yet. This girl knows but she doesn't want to tell."

"Make her tell."

"How?"

The chief appeared to be embarrassed by the question. "Well, what the hell do you want with her if you can't make her talk?" he growled.

"I think she'll talk when we get close enough. The Moslem gang hangs out somewhere near here. The bartender here thinks it might be in the flat of a boy who has a pigeon loft."

"I know where that is!" the sergeant exclaimed. "I searched there."

Everyone, including the prisoners, stared at him. His face reddened. "Now I remember," he said. "There were several boys in the flat. The boy who kept pigeons, Caleb Bowee is his name, lives there with his Grandma; and two of the others roomed there."

"Why the hell didn't you bring them in?" the chief asked.

"I didn't find anything on them to connect them with the Moslem gang or the escaped prisoner," the sergeant said, defending himself. "The boy with the pigeons is a halfwit – he's harmless, and I'm sure the grandma wouldn't put up with a gang in there."

"How in the hell do you know he's harmless?" the chief stormed. "Half the murderers in Sing-Sing look like you and me."

The homicide lieutenant and Anderson exchanged smiles.

"They had two girls with them and –" the sergeant began to explain but the chief wouldn't let him.

"Why in the hell didn't you bring them in, too?"

"What were the girls' names?" Grave Digger asked.

"One was called Sissieratta and –"

"That must be Sissie," Grave Digger said. "It fits. One was Sissie and the other was Sugartit. And one of the boys was Sheik." Turning to Big Smiley, he asked, "What does Sheik look like?"

"Freckle-faced boy the color of a bay horse, with yellow cat eyes," Big Smiley said impassively.

"You're right," the sergeant admitted sheepishly. "He was one of them. I should have trusted my instinct; I started to haul that punk in."

"Well, for God's sake, get the lead out of your ass now," the chief roared. "If you still want to work for the police department."

"Well, Jesus Christ, the other girl, the one Jones calls Sugartit, was Ed Johnson's daughter," the sergeant exploded. "She had one of those souvenir police ID cards signed by yourself and I thought –"

He was interrupted by the flat whacking sound of metal striking against a human skull.

No one had seen Grave Digger move.

What they saw now was Ready Belcher sagging forward with his eyes rolled back into his head and a white cut – not yet beginning to bleed – two inches wide in the black pock-marked skin of his forehead. Big Smiley reared back on the other end of the handcuffs like a dray horse shying from a rattlesnake.

Grave Digger gripped his nickel-plated thirty-eight by the long barrel, making a club out of the butt. The muscles were corded in his rage-swollen neck and his face was distorted with violence. Looking at him, the others were suspended in motion as though turned to stone.

"Stop him, God damn it!" the chief roared. "He'll kill them."

The sculptured figures of the police officers came to life. The sergeant grabbed Grave Digger from behind in a bear hug. Grave Digger doubled over and sent the sergeant flying over his head toward the chief, who ducked in turn and let the sergeant sail on by.

Lieutenant Anderson and the homicide lieutenant converged on Grave Digger from opposite directions. Each grabbed an arm while he was still in a crouch and lifted upward and backward.

Ready was lying prone on the pavement, blood trickling from the dent in his skull, a slack arm drawn tight by the handcuffs attached to Big Smiley's wrist. He looked dead already.

Big Smiley gave the appearance of a terrified blind beggar caught in a bombing raid; his giant frame trembled from head to foot.

Grave Digger had just time enough to kick Ready in the face before the officers jerked him out of range.

"Get him to the hospital, quick!" the chief shouted; and in the next breath added, "Rap him on the head!"

Grave Digger had carried the lieutenants to the ground and it was more than either could to do to follow the chief's command.

The sergeant had already picked himself up and at the chief's order set off at a gallop.

"God damn it, phone for it, don't run after it!" the chief

yelled. "Where the hell is my chauffeur, anyway?"

Cops came running from all directions.

"Give the lieutenants a hand," the chief said. "They've got a wild man."

Four cops jumped into the fray. Finally they pinned Grave Digger to the ground.

The sergeant climbed into the chief's car and began talking into the telephone.

Coffin Ed appeared suddenly. No one had noticed him approaching from his parked car down the street.

"Great God, what's happening, Digger?" he exclaimed.

Everybody was quiet, their embarrassment noticeable.

"What the hell!" he said, looking from one to the other. "What the hell's going on."

Grave Digger's muscles relaxed as though he'd lost consciousness.

"It's just me, Ed," he said, looking up from the ground at his friend. "I just lost my head, is all."

"Let him go," Anderson ordered his helpers. "He's back to normal now."

The cops released Grave Digger and he got to his feet.

"Cooled off now?" the homicide lieutenant asked.

"Yeah. Give me my gun," Grave Digger said.

Coffin Ed looked down at Ready Belcher's bloody head.

"You too, eh, partner," he said. "What did this rebel do?"

"I told him if I caught him holding out on me I'd kill him."

"You told him no lie," Coffin Ed said. Then asked, "Is it that bad?"

"It's dirty, Ed. Galen was a rotten son of a bitch."

"That doesn't surprise me. Have you got anything on it so far?"

"A little, not much."

"What the hell do you want here?" the chief said testily. "I suppose you want to help your buddy beat up some more of your folks."

Grave Digger knew the chief was trying to steer the conversation away from Coffin Ed's daughter, but he didn't know how to help him.

"You two men act as if you want to kill off the whole population of Harlem," the chief kept on.

"You told me to crack down," Grave Digger reminded him.

"Yeah, but I didn't mean in front of my eyes where I would have to be a witness to it."

"It's our beat," Coffin Ed spoke up for his friend. "If you don't like the way we handle it why don't you take us off."

"You're already off," the chief said. "What in the hell did you come back for, anyway?"

"Strictly on private business."

The chief snorted.

"My little daughter hasn't come home and I'm worried about her," Coffin Ed explained. "It's not like her to stay out this late and not let us know where she is."

The chief looked away to hide his embarrassment.

Grave Digger swallowed audibly.

"Hell, Ed, you don't have to worry about Eve," he said in what he hoped was a reassuring tone of voice. "She'll be home soon. You know nothing can happen to her. She's got that police ID card you got for her on her last birthday, hasn't she?"

"I know, but she always phones her mother if she's going to stay out."

"While you're out here looking for her she's probably gone home. Why don't you go back home and go to bed? She'll be all right."

"Jones is telling you right, Ed," the chief said brusquely. "Go home and relax. You're off duty and you're in our way here. Nothing is going to happen to your daughter. You're just having nightmares."

A siren sounded in the distance.

"Here comes the ambulance," Lieutenant Anderson said.

"I'll go and phone home again," Coffin Ed said. "Take it easy, Digger. Don't get yourself docked, too."

As he turned and started off a fusillade of shots sounded

from the upper floor of some nearby tenement. Ten shots from regulation .38 police specials were fired so fast that by the time the sounds had reached the street they were chained together.

Every cop within earshot froze to alert attention. They strained their ears in almost superhuman effort to place the direction from which the shots had come. Their eyes scanned the fronts of the tenements until not a spot escaped their observation.

But no more shots were fired.

The only signs of life left were the lights going out. With the rapidity of gun shots, one light after another went out until only one lighted window remained in the whole block of darkened dingy buildings. It was behind a fire-escape landing on the top floor of the tenement half a block up the street.

All eyes focused on that spot.

The grotesque silhouette of something crawling over the window sill appeared in the glare of light. Slowly it straightened and took the shape of a short, husky man. It staggered slowly along the three feet of grilled iron footing and leaned against the low outer rail. For a moment it swayed back and forth in a macabre pantomime and then, slowly, like a roulette ball climbing the last hurdle before the final slot, it fell over the railing, turned in the air, missed the second landing by a breath. The body turned again and struck the third railing and started to spin faster. It landed with a resounding thud on top of a parked car and lay there with one hand hanging down beside the driver's window as though signaling for a stop.

"Well, God damn it, get going!" the chief shouted in stentorian tone. Then, on second thought, he added, "Not you, Jones. Not you!" and ran toward his car to get his megaphone.

Already motion had broken out. Cops were heading toward the tenement like the Marines landing.

The two cops guarding the entrance ran out into the street

to locate the scene of the disturbance.

The chief grabbed his megaphone and shouted, "Get the lights on that building."

Two spotlights that had been extinguished were turned back on immediately and beamed on the tenement's top floor.

A patrolman stepped from the window onto the fire-escape landing and raised his hands in the light.

"Hold it, everybody!" he shouted. "I want the chief! Is the chief there?"

"Lower the lights," the chief megaphoned. "I'm here. What is it?"

"Send for an ambulance. Petersen is shot –"

"An ambulance is coming."

"Yes sir, but don't let anybody in here yet –"

Grave Digger took hold of Coffin Ed's arm.

"Hang on tight, Ed," he said. "Your daughter's up there."

He felt Coffin Ed's muscles tighten beneath his grip as the cop went on, "We found Pickens but one of the Moslem gangsters grabbed Pete's pistol and shot him. He used his buddy as a shield and I got his buddy but he snatched one of the girls here and escaped into the back room. He's locked himself in there and there's no other way out of this shotgun shack. He says the girl is Detective Ed Johnson's daughter. He threatened to cut her throat if he can't talk to you and Grave Digger Jones. Whatcha want me to do?"

The ambulance approached and the chief had to wait until the siren had died away to make himself heard.

"Has he still got Petersen's pistol?"

"Yes, sir, but he emptied it."

"All right, Officer, sit pat," the chief megaphoned. "We'll get Petersen down the fire escape and I'll go up and see what it's all about."

Coffin Ed's acid-burnt face was hideous with fear.

16

"You stay down here, Johnson," the chief ordered. "I'll take Anderson and Jones."

"Not unless you shoot me," Coffin Ed said.

The chief looked at him.

"Let him come," Grave Digger said.

"I ought to come too; I know the flat," the sergeant said.

"It's my job to come," the lieutenant from homicide said.

"Who the hell's running this police department," the chief said.

"We haven't got any time," Grave Digger replied.

All of them went quickly and quietly as possible. No one spoke again until the chief said through the kitchen door, "All right, I'm the chief. Come out and give yourself up and you won't get hurt."

"How do I know you're the chief?" asked a fuzzy voice from within.

"If you open the door and come out you'll see."

"Don't get so mother-raping smart. You're the chief, but I'm the Sheik."

"Well, all right, you're a big-shot gang boss. What do you want?"

"Keep him talking," Coffin Ed whispered. "I'm going up on the roof."

"Who's that with you?" Sheik asked sharply.

Grave Digger pointed to the sergeant and Lieutenant Anderson.

"The precinct lieutenant and a sergeant," the chief said.

"Where's Grave Digger?"

"He's not here yet. I had to send for him."

"Send those other mother-rapers away. Let's you and me settle this, the Sheik and the Chief."

"How will you know if they're gone if you're scared to come out and look?"

"Let 'em stay then. I don't give a good goddam. And don't think I'm scared. I don't need to take any chances. I got Coffin Ed's daughter by the hair with my left hand and I'm holding a razor-edged butcher knife against her throat with my right hand. If you try to take me I'll cut her mother-raping head off before you can get through the door."

"All right, Sheik, you got us by the short hair, but you know you can't get away. Why don't you come out peaceably and give yourself up like a man. I give you my word that no one will abuse you. The officer you shot ain't seriously hurt. There's no other charge against you. You ought to get off with five years. With time off for good behavior, you'll be back in the big town in three years. Why risk sudden death or the hot seat just for a moment of playing the big shot?"

"Don't hand me that mother-raping crap. You'll hang a kidnapping charge on me for snatching your prisoner."

"What the hell! You can keep him. We don't want him anymore. We found out he didn't kill the man. All he had was a blank pistol."

"So he didn't kill the man?"

"No."

"Who killed him?"

"We don't know yet."

"So you don't know who killed the big Greek, do you?"

"All right, all right, what's that to you? What do you want to get mixed up in something that doesn't concern you?"

"You're one of those smart mother-rapers, ain't you? You're going to be so smart you're going to make me cut her mother-raping throat just to show you."

"Please don't argue with him, Mr. Chief, please," said a small scared voice from within. "He'll kill me. I know he will."

"Shut up!" Sheik said roughly. "I don't need you to tell 'im I'm going to kill you."

Beads of sweat formed on the ridge of the chief's red nose and about the blue bags beneath his eyes.

"Why don't you be a man," he urged, filling his voice with

contempt. "Don't be a mad dog like Vincent Coll. Be a man like Dillinger was. You won't get much. Three years and no more. Don't hide behind an innocent little girl."

"Who the hell do you think you're kidding with that stale crap. This is the Sheik. Can't no dumb cop like you make a fool out of the Sheik. You got the chair waiting for me and you think you're going to kid me into walking out there and sitting in it."

"Don't play yourself too big, punk," the chief said, losing his temper for a moment. "You shot an officer but you didn't kill him. You snatched a prisoner but we don't want him. Now you want to take it out on a little girl who can't defend herself. And you call yourself the Sheik, the big gang leader. You're just a cheap tinhorn punk, yellow to the core."

"Keep on, just keep on. You ain't kidding me with that mother-raping sucker bait. You know it was me who killed him. You've had me tabbed ever since you found out that nigger was shooting blanks."

"What!" The chief was startled. Forgetting himself, he asked Grave Digger, "What the hell's he talking about?"

"Galen." Grave Digger formed the word with his lips.

"Galen!" the chief exclaimed. "You're trying to tell me you killed the white man, you chicken-livered punk?" he roared.

"Keep on, just keep on. You know damn well it was me lowered the boom on the big Greek." He sounded as though he bitterly resented an oversight. "Who do you think you're kidding? You're talking to the Sheik. You think 'cause I'm colored I'm dumb enough to fall for that rock-a-bye-baby crap you're putting down."

The chief had to readjust his train of thought.

"So it was you who killed Galen?"

"He was just the Greek to me," Sheik said scornfully. "Just another gray sucker up here trying to get his kicks. Yeah, I killed him." There was pride in his voice.

"Yeah, it figures," the chief said thoughtfully. "You saw him running down the street and you took advantage of that and shot him in the back. Just what a yellow son of a bitch like you would do. You were probably laying for him and were scared to go out and face him like a man."

"I wasn't laying for the mother-raper no such goddam thing," Sheik said. "I didn't even know he was anywhere about."

"You were nursing a grudge against him."

"I didn't have nothing against the mother-raper. You must be having pipedreams. He was just another gray sucker to me."

"Then why the hell did you shoot him?"

"I was just trying out my new zip gun. I saw the mother-raper running by where I was standing so I just blasted at him to see how good my gun would shoot."

"You God damned little rat," the chief said, but there was more sorrow in his voice than anger. "You sick little bastard. What the God damned hell can be done with somebody like you?"

"I just want you to quit trying to kid me, 'cause I'd just as soon cut this girl's throat right now as not."

"All right, *Mister* Sheik," the chief said in a cold, quiet voice. "What do you want me to do?"

"Is Grave Digger come yet?"

Grave Digger nodded.

"Yeah, he's here, *Mister* Sheik."

"Let him say something then, and you better can that mister crap."

"Eve, this is me, Digger Jones," Grave Digger said, spurning Sheik.

"Answer him," Sheik said.

"Yes, Mr. Jones," she said in a voice so weightless it floated out to the tense group listening like quivering eiderdown.

"Is Sissie in there with you?"

"No, sir, just Granny Bowee and she's sitting in her chair asleep."

"Where's Sissie?"

"She and Inky are in the front room."

"Has he hurt you?"

"Quit stalling," Sheik said dangerously. "I'm going to give you until I count to three."

"Please, Mr. Jones, do what he says. He's going to kill me if you don't."

"Don't worry child, we're going to do what he says," he reassured her and then said, "What do you want, boy?"

"These are my terms: I want the street cleared of cops; all the police blockades moved –"

"What the hell!" the chief exploded.

"We'll do it," Grave Digger said.

"I want to hear the chief say it," Sheik demanded.

"I'll be damned if I will," the chief said.

"Please," came a tiny voice no bigger than a prayer.

"What if she was your daughter," Grave Digger said.

"I'm going to give you until I count three," Sheik said.

"All right, I'll do it," the chief said, sweating blood.

"On your word of honor as a great white man," Sheik persisted.

The chief's red sweating face drained of color.

"All right, all right, on my word of honor," he said.

"Then I want an ambulance driven up to the door downstairs. I want all its doors left open so I can see inside, the back doors and both the side doors, and I want the motor left running."

"All right, all right, what else? The Statue of Liberty?"

"I want this house cleared –"

"All right, all right, I said I'd do that."

"I don't want any mother-raping alarm put out. I don't want anybody to try to stop me. If anybody messes with me before I get away you're going to have a dead girl to bury. I'll put her out somewhere safe when I get clear away, clear out of the state."

"Don't cross him," Grave Digger whispered tensely. "He's teaed to the eyes."

"All right, all right," the chief said. "We'll give you safe passage. If you don't hurt the girl. If you hurt her we won't kill you, but you'll beg us to. Now take five minutes and come out and we'll let you drive away."

"Who do you think you're kidding?" Sheik said. "I ain't that big a fool. I want Grave Digger to come inside of here and put his pistol down on the table, then I'm going to come out."

"You're crazy if you think we're going to give you a pistol," the chief roared.

"Then I'm going to kill her now."

"I'll give it to you," Grave Digger said.

"You're under suspension as of now," the chief said.

"All right," Grave Digger said: then to Sheik, "What do you want me to do?"

"I want you to stand outside the door with the pistol held by the barrel. When I open the door I want you to stick it forward and walk into the room so's the first thing I see is the butt. Then I want you to walk straight ahead and put it on the kitchen table. You got that?"

"Yeah, I got it."

"The rest of you mother-rapers get downstairs," Sheik said.

The two lieutenants and the sergeant looked at the chief for orders.

"All right, Jones, it's your show," the chief said, adding on second thought, "I wish you luck."

He turned and started down the stairs.

The others hesitated. Grave Digger motioned violently for them to leave too. Reluctantly they followed the chief.

It was silent in the kitchen until the sound of the officers' receding footsteps diminished into silence below.

Grave Digger stood facing the kitchen door, holding the pistol as instructed. Sweat poured down his lumpy cordovan-colored face and collected in the collar about his neck.

Finally the sound of movement came from the kitchen. The bolt of the Yale lock clicked open, a hand bolt was pulled back with a grating snap, a chain was unfastened.

The door swung slowly inward.

Only Granny was visible from the doorway. She sat bolt upright in the immobile rocking chair with her hands gripping the arms and her old milky eyes wide open and staring at Grave Digger with a fixed look of fierce disapproval.

Sheik spoke from behind the door, "Turn the butt this way so I can see if it's loaded."

Without looking around, Grave Digger turned the pistol so that Sheik could see the shells in the chambers of the cylinder.

"Go ahead, keep walking," Sheik ordered.

Still without looking around, Grave Digger moved slowly across the room. When he came to the table he looked swiftly toward the small window at the far end of the back wall. It was on the other side of an old-fashioned homemade cupboard which partially blocked the view of the kitchen from the outside, so that only the section between the table and the side wall was visible.

He saw what he was looking for. He leaned slowly forward and placed the pistol on the far side of the table.

"There," he said.

Raising his hands high above his head, he turned slowly away from the table and faced the back wall. He stood so that Sheik had to either pass in front of him to reach the pistol or go around on the other side of the table.

Sheik kicked the door shut, revealing himself and Sugartit, but Grave Digger didn't turn his head or even move his eyes to look at them.

Sheik gripped Sugartit's pony tail tightly in his left hand, pulling her head back hard to make her slender brown throat taut beneath the blade of the butcher knife. They began a slow shuffling walk, like a weird Apache dance in a Montmartre night club.

Sugartit's eyes had the huge liquid look of a dying doe's, and her small brown face looked as fragile as toasted meringue. Her upper lip was sweating copiously.

Sheik kept his gaze pinned on Grave Digger's back while

slowly skirting the opposite walls of the room and approaching the table from the far side. When he came within reach of the pistol he released his hold on Sugartit's pony tail, pressed the knife blade tighter against her throat and reached out with his left hand for the pistol.

Coffin Ed was hanging head downward from the roof, only his head and shoulders visible below the top edge of the kitchen window. He had been hanging there for twenty minutes waiting for Sheik to come into view. He took careful aim at a spot just above Sheik's left ear.

Some sixth sense caused Sheik to jerk his head around at the exact instant Coffin Ed fired.

A third eye, small and black and sightless, appeared suddenly in the exact center of Sheik's forehead between his two startled yellow cat's eyes.

The high-powered bullet had cut only a small round hole in the window glass, but the sound of the shot shattered the whole pane and blasted a shower of glass into the room.

Grave Digger wheeled to catch the fainting girl as the knife clattered harmlessly onto the table top.

Sheik was dead when he started going down. He landed crumpled up beside Granny's immobile rocking chair.

The room was full of cops.

"That was too much of a risk, too much of a risk," Lieutenant Anderson said, shaking his head, a dazed expression of his face.

"What isn't risky on this job?" the chief said authoritatively. "We cops got to take risks."

No one disputed him.

"This is a violent city," he added belligerently.

"There wasn't that much risk," Coffin Ed said. He had his arm about his daughter's trembling shoulders. "They don't have any reflexes when you shoot them in the head."

Sugartit winced.

"Take Eve and go home," Grave Digger said harshly.

"I guess I'd better," Coffin Ed said, limping painfully as he guided Sugartit gently toward the door.

"Geez," a young patrol-car rookie was saying. "Geez. He hung there all that time on just some wire tied around his ankles. I don't know how he stood the pain."

"You'd've stood it too if she was your daughter," Grave Digger said.

"Forget what I said to you about being under suspension, Jones," the chief said.

"I didn't hear you," Grave Digger said.

"Jesus Christ, look at that!" the sergeant exclaimed in amazement. "All that noise and Grandma's still sleeping."

Everybody turned and looked at him. They were solemn for a moment.

"Nothing's ever going to wake her up again," the lieutenant from homicide said. "She must have been dead for hours."

"All right, all right, all right," the chief shouted. "Let's clean up here and get away. We've got this case tied up tighter than Dick's hatband." Then he added in a pleased tone of voice, "That wasn't too difficult, was it?"

17

It was eleven o'clock the next morning.

Inky and Bones had spilled their guts.

It had gone hard for them and when the cops got through with them they were as knotty as fat pine.

The remaining members of the Real Cool Moslems – Camel Mouth, Beau Baby, Punkin Head and Slow Motion – had been rounded up, questioned and were now being held along with Inky and Bones.

Their statements had been practically identical:

They had been standing on the corner of 127th Street and Lenox Avenue.

Q. What for?

A. Just having a dress rehearsal.

Q. What? Dress rehearsal?

A. Yas suh. Like they do on Broadway. We was practicing wearing our new A-rab costumes.

Q. And you saw Mr. Galen when he ran past?

A. Yas suh, that's when we seed him.

Q. Did you recognize him?

A. Naw suh, we didn't know him.

Q. Sheik knew him.

A. Yas suh, but he didn't say he knew 'im and we'd never seen him before.

Q. Choo-Choo must have known him, too.

A. Yas suh, must'ave. Him and Sheik usta room together.

Q. But you saw Sheik shoot him?

A. Yas suh. He said, "Watch this," and pulled out his new zip gun and shot at him.

Q. How many times did he shoot?

A. Just once. That's all a zip gun will shoot.

Q. Yes, these zip guns are single shots. But you knew he had the gun?

A. Yas suh. He'd been working on it for 'most a week.

Q. He made it himself?

A. Yas suh.

Q. Had you ever seen him shoot it previously?

A. Naw suh. It were just finished. He hadn't tried it out.

Q. But you knew he had it on his person?

A. Yas suh. He were going to try it out that night.

Q. And after he shot the white man, what did you do?

A. The man fell down and we went up to see if he'd hit him.

Q. Were you acquainted with the first suspect, Sonny Pickens?

A. Naw suh, we seed him for the first time too when he come past there shootin'.

Q. When you saw the white man had been killed, did you know Sheik had shot him?

A. Naw suh, we thought the other fellow had did it.

Q. Which one of you, er, passed the wind?

A. Suh?

Q. Which one of you broke wind?

A. Oh, that were Choo-Choo, suh, he the one farted.

Q. Was there any special significance in that?

A. Suh?

Q. Why did he do it?

A. That were just a salute we give to the cops.

Q. Oh! Was the perfume throwing part of it?

A. Yas suh, when they got mad Caleb thew the perfume on them.

Q. To allay their anger, er, ah, make them jolly?

A. Naw suh, to make them madder.

Q. Oh! Well, why did Sheik kidnap Pickens, the other suspect?

A. Just to put something over on the cops. He hated cops.

Q. Why?

A. Suh?

Q. Why did he hate cops? Did he have any special reason to hate cops?

A. Special reason? To hate cops? Naw suh. He didn't need none. Just they was cops, is all.

Q. Ah, yes, just they was cops. Is this the zip gun Sheik had?

A. Yas suh. Leastwise it looks like it.

Q. How did Bones come to be in possession of it?

A. He gave it to Bones when he was running off. Bones's old man work for the city and he figgered it was safe with Bones.

Q. That's all for you, boy. You had better be scared.

A. Ah is.

That was the case. Open and shut.

Sonny Pickens could not be implicated in the murder. He was being held temporarily on a charge of disturbing the peace while a district attorney's assistant was studying the New York State criminal code to see what other charge could be lodged against him for shooting a citizen with a blank gun.

His friends, Lowtop Brown and Rubberlips Wilson had been hauled in as suspicious persons.

The cases of the two girls had been referred to the probation officers, but as yet nothing had been done. Both were supposedly at their respective homes, suffering from shock.

The bullet had been removed from the victim's brain and given to the ballistics bureau. No further autopsy was required. Mr. Galen's daughter, Mrs. Helen Kruger of Wading River, Long Island, had claimed the body for burial.

The bodies of the others, Granny and Caleb, Choo-Choo and Sheik, lay unclaimed in the morgue. Perhaps the Baptist church in Harlem, of which Granny was a member, would give her a decent Christian burial. She had no life insurance and it would be financially inconvenient for the church, unless the members contributed to defray the costs.

Caleb would be buried along with Sheik and Choo-Choo in potters field, unless the medical college of one of the universities obtained their bodies for dissection. No college would want Choo-Choo's, however, because it had been too badly damaged.

Ready Belcher was in Harlem Hospital, in the same ward where Charlie Richardson, whose arm had been chopped off, had died earlier. His condition was serious, but he would live. He would never look the same, however, and should his teenage whore ever see him again she wouldn't recognize him.

Big Smiley and Reba were being held for contributing to the delinquency of minors, manslaughter, operating a house of prostitution, and sundry other charges.

The woman who was shot in the leg by Coffin Ed was in Knickerbocker Hospital. Two ambulance-chasing shysters were vying with each other for her consent to sue Coffin Ed and the New York police department on a fifty-fifty split of the judgement, but her husband was holding out for a sixty-percent cut.

That was the story; the second and corrected story. The late editions of the morning newspapers had gone hog wild with it:

The prominent New York Citizen hadn't been shot, as first reported, by a drunken Negro who had resented his presence in a Harlem bar. No, not at all. He had been shot to death by a teenage Harlem gangster called Sheik, who was the leader of a teenage gang called the Real Cool Moslems. Why? Well, Sheik had wanted to find out if his zip gun would actually shoot.

The copy writers used a book of adjectives to describe the bizarre aspects of the three-ring Harlem murder; meanwhile they tossed a bone of commendation to the brave policemen who had worked through the small hours of the morning, tracking down the killer in the Harlem jungle and shooting him to death in his lair less than six hours after the fatal shot had been fired.

The headlines read:

POLICE PUT HEAT ON REAL COOL MOSLEMS
DEATH IS THE KISS-OFF FOR THRILL KILL
HARLEM MANIAC RUNS AMUCK

But already the story was a thing of the past, as dead as the four main characters.

"Kill it," ordered the city editor of an afternoon paper. "Someone else has already been murdered somewhere else."

Uptown in Harlem, the sun was shining on the same drab scene it illuminated every other morning at eleven o'clock. No one missed the few expendable colored people being held on various charges in the big new granite skycraper jail on Centre Street that had replaced the old New York City tombs.

In the same building, in a room high up on the southwest corner, with a fine clear view of the Battery and North River, all that remained of the case was being polished off.

Earlier the police commissioner and the chief of police had had a heart-to-heart talk about possible corruption in the Harlem branch of the police department.

"There are strong indications that Galen was protected by some influential person up there, either the police department or in the city government," the police commissioner said.

"Not in the department," the chief maintained. "In the first place, that low license number of his – UG-Sixteen – tells me he had friends higher up than a precinct captain, because that kind of license number is issued only to the specially privileged, and that don't even include me."

"Did you find any connections with politicians in that area?"

"Not connecting Galen; but the woman, Reba, telephoned a colored councilman this morning and ordered him to get down here and get her out on bail."

The commissioner sighed. "Perhaps we'll never know the extent of Galen's activities up there."

"Maybe not, but one thing we do know," the chief said. "The son of a bitch is dead, and his money won't corrupt anybody else."

Afterward the police commissioner reviewed the suspension of Coffin Ed. Grave Digger and Lieutenant Anderson were present along with the chief at this conference. Coffin Ed had exercised his privilege to be absent.

"In the light of subsequent developments in this case, I am inclined to be lenient toward Detective Johnson," the commissioner said. "His compulsion to fire at the youth is understandable, if not justifiable, in view of his previous unfortunate experience with an acid thrower." The commissioner had come into office by way of a law practice and could handle those jaw-breaking words with much greater ease than the cops, who'd learned their trade pounding beats.

"What's your opinion, Jones?" he asked.

Grave Digger turned from his customary seat, one ham propped on the window ledge and one foot planted on the floor, and said, "Yes sir, he's been touchy and on edge ever since that con-man threw the acid in his eyes, but he was never rough on anybody in the right."

"Hell, I wasn't disciplining Johnson so much as I was just taking the weight off the whole God damned police department," the chief said in defense of his action. "We'd have caught holy hell from all the sob sisters, male and female, in this town if those punks had turned out to be innocent pranksters."

"So you are in favor of his reinstatement?" the commissioner asked.

"Why not?" the chief said. "If he's got the jumps let him work them off on those hoodlums up in Harlem who gave them to him."

"Right ho," the commissioner said, then turned to Grave Digger again: "Perhaps you can tell me, Jones; one aspect of the case has me puzzled. All of the reports state that there was a huge crowd of people present at the victim's death, and witnessed the actual shooting. One report states –" he fumbled among the papers on his desk until he found the page he wanted. " 'The street was packed with people for a distance of two blocks when deceased met death by gunfire.' Why is this? Why do the people up in Harlem congregate at the scene of a killing as though it were a three-ring circus?"

"It is," Grave Digger said tersely. "It's the greatest show on earth."

"That happens everywhere," Anderson said. "People will congregate at a killing wherever it takes place."

"Yes, of course, out of morbid curiosity. But I don't mean that exactly. According to reports, not only the reports on this case, but all reports that have come into my office, this, er, phenomenon, let us say, is more evident in Harlem that any place else. What do you think, Jones?"

"Well, it's like this, Commissioner," Grave Digger said. "Every day in Harlem, two and three times a day, the colored people see some colored man being chased by another colored man with a knife or an axe or a club. Or else being chased by a white cop with a gun, or by a white man with his fists. But it's only once in a blue moon they get to see a white man being chased by one of them. A big white man at that. That was an event. A chance to see some white blood spilled for a change, and spilled by a black man, at that. That was greater than Emancipation Day. As they say up in Harlem, that was the greatest. That's what Ed and I are always up against when we try to make Harlem safe for white people."

"Perhaps I can explain it," the commissioner said.

"Not to me," the chief said drily. "I ain't got the time to listen. If the folks up there want to see blood, they're going to see all the blood they want if they kill another white man."

"Jones is right," Anderson said. "But it makes for trouble."

"Trouble!" Grave Digger echoed. "All they know up there is trouble. If trouble was money, everybody in Harlem would be a millionaire."

The telephone rang. The commissioner picked up the receiver.

"Yes . . .? Yes, send him up." He replaced the receiver and said, "It's the ballistics report. It's coming up."

"Fine," the chief said. "Let's write it in the record and close this case up. It was a dirty business from start to finish and I'm sick and God damned tired of it."

"Right ho," the commissioner said.

Someone knocked.

"Come in," he said.

The lieutenant from homicide who had worked on the case came in and placed the zip gun and the battered lead pellet taken from the murdered man's brain on the commissioner's desk.

The commissioner picked up the gun and examined it curiously.

"So this is a zip gun?"

"Yes sir. It's made from an ordinary toy cap pistol. The barrel of the toy pistol is sawed off and this four-inch section of heavy brass pipe is fitted in in its place. See, it's soldered to the frame, then for greater stability it's bound with adjustable cables in place. The shell goes directly into the barrel, then this clip is inserted to prevent it from backfiring. The firing pin is soldered to the original hammer. On this one it's made from the head and a quarter-inch section of an ordinary Number Six nail, filed down to a point."

"It is more primitive than I had imagined, but it is certainly ingenious."

The others looked at it with bored indifference; they had seen zip guns before.

"And this will project a bullet with sufficient force to kill a man, to penetrate his skull?"

"Yes sir."

"Well, well, so this is the gun which killed Galen and led the boy who made it to be killed in turn."

"No sir, not this gun."

"What!"

Everybody sat bolt upright, eyes popping and mouths open. Had the lieutenant said the Empire State Building had been stolen and smuggled out of town, he couldn't have caused a greater sensation.

"What do you mean, not that gun!" the chief roared.

"That's what I came to tell you," the lieutenant said. "This gun fires a twenty-two caliber bullet. It contained the case of a twenty-two shell when the sergeant found it. Galen was killed with a thirty-two caliber fired from a more powerful pistol."

"This is where we came in," Anderson said.

"I'll be God damned if it is!" the chief bellowed like an enraged bull. "The papers have already gotten the story that he was killed with this gun and they've gone crazy with it. We'll be the laughingstock of the world."

"No," the commissioner said quietly but firmly. "We have made a mistake, that is all."

"I'll be God damned if we have," the chief said, his face turning blood red with passion. "I say the son of a bitch was killed with that gun and that punk lying in the morgue killed him, and I don't give a God damn what ballistics show."

The commissioner looked solemnly from face to face. There was no question in his eyes, but he waited for someone else to speak.

"I don't think it's worth re-opening the case," Lieutenant Anderson said. "Galen wasn't a particularly lovable character."

"Lovable or not, we got the killer and that's the gun and that's that," the chief said.

"Can we afford to let a murderer go free?" the chief said.

The commissioner looked again from face to face.

"This one," Grave Digger said harshly. "He did a public service."

"That's not for us to determine, is it?" the commissioner said.

"You'll have to decide that, sir," Grave Digger said. "But if you assign me to look for the killer, I resign."

"Er, what? Resign from the force?"

"Yes sir. I say the killer will never kill again and I'm not going to track him down to pay for this killing even if it costs me my job."

"Who killed him, Jones?"

"I couldn't say, sir."

The commissioner looked grave. "Was he as bad as that?"

"Yes sir."

The commissioner looked at the lieutenant from homicide.

"But this zip gun was fired, wasn't it?"

"Yes sir. But I've checked with all the hospitals and the precinct station in Harlem and there has been no gunshot injury reported."

"Someone could have been injured who was afraid to report it."

"Yes sir. Or the bullet might have landed harmlessly against a building or an automobile."

"Yes. But there are the other boys who are involved. They might be indicted for complicity. If it is proved that they were his accomplices, they face the maximum penalty for murder."

"Yes sir," Anderson said. "But it's been pretty well established that the murder – or rather the action of the boy firing the zip gun – was not premeditated. And the others knew nothing of his intention to fire at Galen until it was too late to prevent him."

"According to their statements."

"Well, yes sir. But it's up to us to accept their statements or have them bound over to the grand jury for indictment. If we don't charge complicity when they go up for arraignment the court will only fine them for disturbing the peace."

The commissioner looked back at the lieutenant from homicide. "Who else knows about this?"

"No one outside of this office, sir. They never had the gun in ballistics; they only had the bullet."

"Shall we put it to a vote?" the commissioner asked.

No one said anything.

"The ayes have it," the commissioner said. He picked up the small lead pellet that had murdered a man. "Jones, there is a flat roof on a building across the park. Do you think you can throw this so it will land there?"

"If I can't sir, my name ain't Don Newcombe," Grave Digger said.

18

The old stone apartment house at 2702 Seventh Avenue was heavy with pseudo-Greek trimmings left over from the days when Harlem was a fashionable white neighbourhood and the Negro slums were centred around San Juan Hill on West 42nd Street.

Grave Digger pushed open the cracked glass door and

searched for the name of Coolie Dunbar among the row of mail boxes nailed to the front hall wall. He found the name on a fly-specked card, followed by the apartment number 3-B.

The automatic elevator, one of the first made, was out of order.

He climbed the dark ancient stairs to the third floor and knocked on the left-hand door at the front.

A middle-aged brown-skinned woman with a worried expression opened the door and said, "Coolie's at work and we've told the people already we'll come in and pay our rent in the office when –"

"I'm not the rent collector, I'm a detective," Grave Digger said, flashing his badge.

"Oh!" The worried expression turned to one of apprehension. "You're Mr. Johnson's partner. I thought you were finished with her."

"Almost. May I talk to her?"

"I don't see why you got to keep on bothering her if you ain't got nothing on Mr. Johnson's daughter," she complained as she guarded the entrance. "They were both in it together."

"I'm not going to arrest her. I would just like to ask her a few questions to clear up the last details."

"She's in bed now."

"I don't mind."

"All right," she consented grudgingly. "Come on in. But if you've got to arrest her, then keep her. Me and Coolie have been disgraced enough by that girl. We're respectable church people –"

"I'm sure of it," he cut her off. "But she's your niece, isn't she?"

"She's Coolie's niece. I haven't got any wild ones in my family."

"You're lucky," he said.

She pursed her lips and opened a door next to the kitchen.

"Here's a policeman to see you, Sissie," she said.

Grave Digger entered the small bedroom and closed the door behind him.

Sissie lay on a narrow single bed with the covers pulled up to her chin. At sight of Grave Digger her red, tear-swollen eyes grew wide with terror.

He drew up the single hard-backed chair and sat down.

"You're a very lucky little girl," he said. "You have just missed being a murderer."

"I don't know what you mean," she said in a terrified whisper.

"Listen," he said. "Don't lie to me. I'm dog-tired and you children have already made me as depressed as I've ever been. You don't know what kind of hell it is sometimes to be a cop."

She watched him like a half-wild kitten poised for flight.

"I didn't kill him. Sheik killed him," she whispered.

"We know Sheik killed him," he said in a flat voice. He looked weary beyond words. "Listen, I'm not here as a cop. I'm here as a friend. Ed Johnson is my closest friend and his daughter is your closest friend. That ought to make us friends too. As a friend I tell you we've got to get rid of the gun."

She hesitated, debating with herself, then said quickly before she could change her mind, "I threw it down a water drain on 128th Street near Fifth Avenue."

He sighed. "That's good enough. What kind of gun was it?"

"It was a thirty-two. It had the picture of an owl's head on the handle and Uncle Coolie called it an Owl's Head."

"Has he missed it?"

"He missed it out of the drawer this morning when he started for work and asked Aunt Cora if she'd moved it. But he ain't said nothing to me yet. He was late for work and I think he wanted to give me all day to put it back."

"Does he need it in his work?"

"Oh no, he works for a garage in the Bronx."

"Good. Does he have a permit for it?"

"No, sir. That's what he's so worried about."

"Okay. Now listen. When he asks you about it tonight, you tell him you took it to protect yourself against Mr. Galen and that during the excitement you left it in Sheik's room. Tell him that I found it there but I don't know to whom it belongs. He won't say any more about it."

"Yes sir. But he's going to be awfully mad."

"Well, Sissie, you can't escape all punishment."

"No, sir."

"Why did you shoot at Mr. Galen anyway? You can tell me now since it doesn't matter."

"It wasn't account of myself," she said. "It was on account of Sugartit – Evelyn Johnson. He was after her all the time and I was afraid he was going to get her. She tries to be wild and does crazy things sometimes and I was afraid he was going to get her and do to her what he did to me. That would ruin her. She ain't an orphan like me with nobody to really care what happens to her; she's from a good family with a father and a mother and a good home and I wasn't going to let him ruin her."

He sat there listening to her, a big, tough lumpy-faced cop, looking as though he might cry.

"How'd you plan to do it?" he asked.

"Oh, I was just going to shoot him. I'd made a date with him at the Inn for me and Sugartit, but I wasn't going to take her. I was going to make him drive me out somewhere in his car by telling him we were going to pick her up; and then I was going to shoot him and run away. I took Uncle Coolie's pistol and hid it downstairs in the hall in a hole in the plaster so I could get it when I went out. But before time came for me to go, Sugartit came by here. I wasn't expecting her and I couldn't tell her I wanted to go out, so it was late before I could get rid of her. I left her at the subway at 125th Street, thinking she was going home, then I ran all the way over to Lenox to meet Mr. Galen; but when I got over on Lenox I saw all the commotion going on. Then I saw him come running down the street and Sonny chasing him and shooting at him with a gun. It looked like half the people in

Harlem were running after him. I got in the crowd and followed and when I caught up with him at 127th Street I saw that Sonny was going to shoot at him again, so I shot at him, too. I don't think anyone even saw me shoot; everybody was looking at Sonny. But when I saw him fall and all the Moslems in their costumes run up and ganged up around him I was scared one of them was going to see me, so I ran around the block and threw the gun in a drain, then came back to Caleb's from the other way and made out like I didn't know what had happened. I didn't know then that Caleb had been shot."

"Have you told anyone else about this?"

"No sir. When I saw Sugartit come sneaking into Caleb's, I was going to tell her I'd shot him because I knew she'd come back looking for him. But Choo-Choo had let it slip out that Sheik was carrying his zip gun, and then after Sonny said his gun wouldn't shoot anything but blanks I knew right away it was Sheik who'd shot him; and I was scared to say anything."

"Good. Now listen to me. Don't tell anybody else. I won't tell anybody either. We'll just keep it to ourselves, our own private secret. Okay?"

"Yes sir. You can bet I won't tell anybody else. I just want to forget it – if I ever can."

"Good. I don't suppose there's any need to tell you to keep away from bad company; you ought to have learned your lesson by now."

"I'm going to do that, I promise."

"Good. Well, Sissie," Grave Digger said, getting slowly to his feet, "you made your bed hard; if it hurts lying on it, don't complain."

It was visiting hour next day in the Centre Street jail.

Sissie said, "I brought you some cigarettes, Sonny. I didn't know whether you had a girl to bring you any."

"Thanks," Sonny said. "I ain't got no girl."

"How long do you think they'll give you?"

"Six months, I suppose."
"That much. Just for what you did."
"They don't like for people to shoot at anybody, even if you don't hit them, or even if they ain't shooting nothing but blanks like what I did."
"I know," she said sympathetically. "Maybe you're getting off easy at that."
"I ain't complaining," Sonny said.
"What are you going to do when you get out?"
"Go back to shining shoes, I suppose."
"What's going to happen to your shine parlor?"
"Oh, I'll lose that one, but I'll get me another one."
"You got a car?"
"I had one but I couldn't keep up the payments and the man took it back."
"You need a girl to look after you."
"Yeah, who don't? What you going to do yourself, now that your boy friend's dead?"
"I don't know. I just want to get married."
"That shouldn't be hard for you."
"I don't know anybody who'll have me."
"Why not?"
"I've done a lot of bad things."
"Like what?"
"I'd be ashamed to tell you everything I've done."
"Listen, to show you I ain't scared of nothing you might have done, I want you to be my girl."
"I don't want to play around any more."
"Who's talking about playing around. I'm talking about for keeps."
"I don't mind. But there's something I've got to tell you first. It's about me and Sheik."
"What about you and Sheik?"
"I'm going to have a baby by the time you get out of jail."
"Well, that makes it different," he said. "We'd better get married right away. I'll talk to the man and ask him to see if he can't arrange it."

ABOUT THE AUTHOR

CHESTER HIMES was born in Missouri in 1909. He began writing while serving a prison sentence for a jewel theft and published just short of twenty novels before his death in 1984. Among his best-known thrillers are *Cotton Comes to Harlem, The Real Cool Killers,* and *The Heat's On,* all available from Vintage.

Printed in the United States
by Baker & Taylor Publisher Services